Their Agency Fathers

Ron Wootters

"Their Agency Fathers" ISBN 1-58939-348-1 (softcover version).

Published 2003 by Virtualbookworm.com Publishing Inc., P.O. Box 9949,
College Station, TX , 77842, US. ©2002, 2003 Ron Wootters. All rights
reserved. No part of this publication may be reproduced, stored in a retrieval
system, or transmitted in any form or by any means, electronic, mechanical,
recording or otherwise, without the prior written permission of Ron Wootters.

Manufactured in the United States of America

To: Rosemary & Joan

ACKNOWLEDGMENTS

Sincerest thanks to my Wife and Sister, who took the time to proofread this novel.

PROLOGUE

It's going to be another beautiful day in Jamaica. The usual morning shower has just ended and the sun is already out again, drying up the moisture on the roads and sidewalks, as an American man walks down a street in the poorer part of Kingston. As he approaches a small hotel, he slows his pace and checks out his surroundings. He should not be under surveillance for any reason, but one never knows.

He stops next to a tree and removes a pack of cigarettes from his inside pocket, takes one out, puts it in his mouth and lights it. During this process, he has been checking the area to his left and to the rear for any person or persons that may be following. After he has taken several puffs, and feels sure no one is following, the man continues to the hotel.

Upon entering the front door, he finds himself in the lobby. It is small and very old, but quaint. As he scans the area, a Spanish-looking man approaches him from his left rear. The American senses his presence and turns in that direction.

"Do you always sneak up on people?" the American inquires.

"Yes," answers the man, with no further explanation. He then motions for the American to follow him. The two men walk down a hall that leads to what looks like a back porch, where tables and chairs are set up. They seat themselves at a table on the far end of the porch and order two coffees. Once alone, they continue their conversation.

"Did you notice anyone suspicious on your way here?" inquires the Latino man.

"No," is the answer.

"Are you sure?" the Latino presses.

"I have been doing this type of thing long enough to spot surveillance," the American insists.

"Do you have the information?"

"Do you have the money?" asks the American.

"Yes."

The two men decide to use the small breakfast menus to make the trade, and after their coffee arrives, they engage in conversation. During their talk, first one and then the other place letter-size envelopes inside their menus. That done, they quickly survey the area for other people, and then push the menus across the table to one another. Additional conversation follows for a brief time, then a suggestion to leave. Both men agree, and while gathering up cigarette packs and lighters, the envelopes are also retrieved and placed alongside them in their inside pockets.

"I have done this many times," says the American, "but I still get a rush at this point, knowing that if I am being watched, this will be the time they'll arrest me."

"You are lucky," the Latino informs him. "If I caught a man doing what you are doing, I would just blow his brains out."

"I just do it for the money, that's all. No political reasons or anything," the American reassures the man.

"I don't care why you are doing it; you are still a traitor to your country."

"I guess it's time to leave," the American says, and both men stand to walk back to the lobby area, where they say goodbye. The Latino watches from a side window as the other man walks down the sidewalk. He shakes his head as he thinks about the man's defense: *I just do it for the money, that's all.*

That is the very reason that disgusts him.

CHAPTER ONE

Shadows reflect against the seawall as two men drag their rubber raft across the beach of a country hostile to Uncle Sam. This is just one of many missions they have been on together, but in their minds neither can figure out why it had to be done tonight-and with a full moon, no less. After all, these targets aren't that important, but they *are* very dangerous.

After securing their raft, the two men proceeded to their separate objectives. That's another thing bouncing around in their minds: Why the second objective? The first objective seems insignificant enough, but the second is even worse. They guess it's standard reasoning back at HQ: *The dumb leading the dumber.*

First one, then the other, disappears from the beach. It's a still night, but the moon is so bright it seems as though it should be a busy mid-afternoon.

All of a sudden, it *is* like a busy afternoon-busy as a celebration of the Chinese New Year. Out of nowhere come muzzle flashes from automatic weapons and commands being shouted: "Kill the Yankee Dogs!"

That must be us, the two men think as they both beat a hasty retreat back to the beach. The gunfire is so intense that anything over three feet tall is being cut down.

Both men look at each other on the beach without saying a word. They have been set up, and they both know it. Outnumbered ten to one, and no way of escaping. Someone had thought of everything…or had they?

There are actually two things someone had neglected to consider. One was pissing off two old farts that had been around the block so many times they had streets named after them…and the other was the quarter-pound sticks of C-4 explosives they both had in their packs. As they unpacked the explosives, they discussed their options on how to use it.

"We could throw it at them, and while they're regrouping make our getaway with the raft," Jar Head offers.

"No, that wouldn't work," answers Doggie, "they would just machine-gun us and the rubber raft before we got out of range."

"How about if we crawl out, bury the explosives, and play dead, and when they come over to check us, the explosives will cream them?"

"No, that won't work either," Jar Head replies. "We would have to set them off with the timers, and if we guess wrong we'll be shit out of luck."

"Well, that leaves only one alternative." Both men say at the same time: "We attack."

"Don't get too excited and shoot me by mistake, ya dickhead Doggie," Jar Head instructs.

"Don't worry about that," Doggie reassures him. "I'll take special care not to. I want to be very calm when I shoot you, so I don't have to shoot you twice."

Both men smile before they start to crawl in opposite directions. No plan is necessary for these two; they have been working as a team for so long that one just about knows what the other is going to do before it happens. In this case, they will attack at an angle from opposite sides. First with explosives, then automatic weapons, hand guns, knives... and if all that fails, they will employ the old Ninja technique: *reach into your shorts, get a handful and blind the enemy with a shower of shit as you make a hasty retreat.*

Jar Head is not quite in the position he would like to be, but it will have to do because Doggie has just started the show with a stick of C-4. As all the guns of the opposition swing in the direction of the explosion, Jar Head makes his move. *I can't believe how close I'm getting without being discovered. I guess they're in shock,* he thought. *A detachment of 20 being attacked by two.*

All guns are firing in Doggie's direction as Jar Head sets the timers on two sticks of C-4. *Now, the trick to this is not to get involved in a volleyball game with the enemy when you throw the C-4.* Jar Head takes a deep breath, then throws the two bundles of explosives, watching as long as he dares before they detonate. Just before the C-4 explodes, he takes cover behind a large palm tree.

A second after the explosions erupt, Jar Head and Doggie come up firing at their would-be assassins.

The enemy troops are either dead or dazed from the explosions, and with two automatic weapons blazing at them, the fight-or-flee syndrome comes into play...with most deciding on the latter.

After faking a pursuit of the enemy, the attackers decide to head for the raft. As they return to the beach, Doggie registers a complaint.

"You took long enough to do something. I thought maybe you

took off with the raft while I held off the troops."

"No," Jar Head replies," I was just trying to get a clear shot at you, but I couldn't. I guess you were hiding in a hole until I kicked all of their asses."

Without hesitation, the two men remove additional C-4 bundles from their packs and set the timers.

"Four minutes?" inquires Doggie.

"Sounds about right," Jar Head confirms.

When all of the timers are set, the bundles are tossed back into the tree line at different intervals, and the men take off with the raft in tow.

The raft has just cleared the breakwater when the regrouped detachment starts showing up on the beach. As they begin to fire at the raft, a series of explosions erupts from behind their positions on the beach. Between the force of the explosions and the debris flying across the beach, the detachment's assault is again broken up as the raft extends and escapes.

As the two men row to the pickup point they reflect on what had just happened. *It was a set-up, but by who? Is it one of our people? Someone who has access to our operations? Or both? Maybe Swabbie will have some ideas on this one.*

***

It is early spring in Washington, D. C. Everyone is out walking in the noonday sun, and full of good cheer now that winter is again behind them.

Well, everyone is in good cheer if you don't count Doggie and Jar Head. They are both in a black mood as they walk down the hall to their boss's office. He used to be the third man of their team, back in the Cold War days; then he got promoted to an in-house position and a pussy job, as they like to point out to him. Now, he's the Section Chief of Special Projects…but he's still Swabbie to them.

This was a highly classified Section, until all the changes were made: the Director of CIA appointed from the civilian or political military arena, the congressional oversight committee and their staff. Once these changes went into effect, every time an important clandestine plan was submitted to Congress, the Agency had to work fast as hell to get it completed before they read about it in the newspapers.

Swabbie once suggested at a high level meeting that banana peels be spread in the hallways during Congressional clandestine briefings-this in the interest of slowing, or hopefully injuring, anyone rushing to report to their local KGB rep or the New York Times.'

In most cases, anyone in Doggie or Jar Head's frame of mind

would walk past the secretary and barge into the boss's office.

But in most cases, you don't have a secretary like Gert standing guard outside it. Gert was a pleasant and charming lady, but if you crossed her she might kick your ass. She once, armed with only an umbrella, chased a would-be mugger five blocks before he got away.

Gert claims she would have gotten him, but it started to rain and she lost traction.

"Good morning," Gert sings out as Doggie and Jar Head approach her desk.

"Hi, Gert," both men grumble.

"Well, aren't we both in a good mood this morning?" Gert observes.

"Yeah, we are!" Jar Head barks. "Is Swabbie in?"

"Boy it must be serious if you're going to bypass the ration of bullshit you both usually give me," Gert says as she buzzes Swabbie's intercom.

"What is it, Gert?" a voice replies.

"It's the Dynamic Duo, sir."

"Send them in."

"We'll give you a double ration next time, Gert", both men promise as they enter the office.

"Don't be surprised if I have my umbrella handy," Gert whips back with a smile as the door closes.

Jar Head starts off the meeting with a brief inquiry.

"Okay, what the fuck is going on?"

"What do you mean?" their boss inquires.

"What do I mean!" replies Jar Head. "Those guys waiting for us on the beach had printed programs of the night's activities."

"I can't believe that," answers a surprised Swabbie.

"It's true!" Doggie tells him. "It was an ambush, and it had our names written all over it."

"How could that be?"

"I don't know *how*, but I have a feeling about *whom*. One of those political bastards on the Oversight Committee, or one of their staff members, should be considered as front runners," snaps Jar Head.

"But how could they get that far inside, to get you sent on a mission, and then set you both up?" asks Swabbie. "And why would they want you dead?"

"How long ago was the plan hatched?" inquires Doggie.

"Come to think of it," Swabbie realizes, "I don't remember anything being on your plate."

"In the past three months, how many times were you out of the office?" inquires Jar Head.

Swabbie thumbs through his desk calendar quickly to double-check his memory. "I took a week off two months ago, and I just got back from a two-week trip to France."

"I'd say, since someone at your level has to give extremely advanced notice when requesting time off, whoever is behind this had access to your requests and proposed the plan your first week off, then somehow got the priority raised and it was rushed it into operation during your second week in France," offers Jar Head. "Doing it that way, they made sure you wouldn't find out about it and put a stop to it."

"Swabbie, it looks like you have some investigating to do," Doggie says. "Somebody up the line had to be involved to push the project through with such short notice."

"How were you briefed?" asks Swabbie.

"On the fly," answers Doggie, "but that's not unusual; the target was unusual. We both questioned it, but being on the fly and with the briefer not having much more than a basic package of info, the questions went unanswered."

Swabbie is very intent as the three continue their conversation.

As Doggie and Jar Head finish up their debriefing about the mission--including the big-ass full moon--Swabbie is in deep thought, looking at his calendar.

Jar Head and Doggie look at each other, then at the Section Chief, "What is it?" asks Doggie.

"I'm just trying to come up with a reason why someone would want you out of the way that badly,"

"Anything come to mind?" Jar Head inquires.

"There is one item, but I can't believe anyone would go to those lengths," Swabbie says in disbelief.

"Let's talk about it," offers Doggie as he and Jar Head take a seat in front of his desk.

"Well, the only thing that comes to mind," Swabbie begins, "are suggestions that you two are getting too long in the tooth for these types of missions, and should be replaced by younger men." "I've been fighting them off, but a certain Army general with high political ties keeps pushing, and also wants to supply the replacements."

"This could get very interesting," Jar Head observes, and the other two agree as they continue their analysis of the situation.

Two hours have passed, and Swabbie is scheduled for a high-level meeting and has to call the session to an end.

"Why don't we take the ladies out to dinner this evening?" Swabbie suggests.

"Sounds good," the other two confirm as they follow Swabbie out of his office.

"So, Gert, what is it?" asks Jar Head.

"What is what?" asks Gert

"What?" replies Jar Head

Gert looks at Jar Head and says, "I didn't think that double dose of bullshit was going to show up so soon."

"You can borrow my umbrella, Gert," Swabbie offers as he continues out of the area. "It's in my office."

***

The warmth of the spring day has given way to the coolness of an early spring evening, as Swabbie's Lincoln town car pulls up to the valet parking at Harvey's Seafood Restaurant in downtown Washington, D.C. Jar Head is the first to exit the car; he gets out of the front passenger seat and turns back to help Swabbie's wife out as she slides across the front seat.

Once Swabbie's wife Anne is out, he opens the rear door and helps his girl Mims out, and Swabbie does the same for Doggie's girl Jessie on the other side of the car. With all of the ladies outside, Jar Head looks into the back seat and says, "Hey, lady, do you need any help?"

"No, no, I can get out on my own," replies Doggie as he flips Jar Head a clandestine bird. Both men smile as they join the others on their way to the front door.

Once inside, they are greeted by the manager of the restaurant, who also happens to be one of Swabbie's friends. After the manager greets the party, he shows them to one of the best tables in the house.

After everyone has ordered their cocktails and the waiter leaves to retrieve the drinks, Jar Head starts to lecture Anne.

"Now, Anne, I don't want you to cause a scene while you're here."

"What do you mean?" Anne fires back. She has known Jar Head and Doggie for many years, and is always prepared for anything.

"The silverware," Jar Head says quietly.

"You'll never let me forget that, will you?"

"Just trying to keep you and your husband, the Swab Jockey here, out of a scandalous situation."

"Scandalous situation," repeats Anne. "Do you know what he's talking about?" Anne motions to the other two women. Both Mims and Jessie admit they don't know.

"Well, some years ago I suggested we invite these two bozos to come here with us for dinner. My honey and I had lobster, and these two ordered Philly cheese steaks or something, I forget. When we had finished our meals, I mentioned to my honey that the little pick I used to eat the lobster would come in handy at home, and I wondered if I could borrow it for a while.

"'No, no,' he says, 'you can't take that.' Like letting me borrow that pick was going to make this place go under."

"So you didn't get to borrow the pick, then?" inquires Jessie.

"No, I borrowed it when he wasn't looking," answers Anne, "then these two squealed on me when we were getting ready to leave the restaurant and he made me put it back."

"What a rat," Mims says as she pokes Jar Head with her elbow. "You know squealers never prosper."

"You can say that again; look at my date" responds Doggie.

"Oh, is that right," snaps Jessie. "I think I'll have the lobster."

"Me too," adds Mims.

"It does sound good." Anne pauses. "I think I will too."

"See what you started?" Swabbie says to Jar Head. "With any luck, we should be on the front page of the morning paper."

"We'll watch them," Doggie promises. "We work in the field, you know."

"Yeah, we don't have one of those in-house pussy jobs," comments Jar Head.

The evening continues in normal fashion, with laughing and good conversation…and Doggie and Jar Head watching every move the ladies make. They even held off going to the bathroom for as long as they could, so both of them would be at the table at the same time. That part wasn't easy, with the ladies ordering them drink after drink and saying, "It's okay to have another; Swabbie is driving."

When dinner is completed, Anne suggests they go to her house for coffee, and the ladies seem overjoyed by the invitation. After paying the bill, the party goes outside to wait for a valet to get the car.

After a short wait the Lincoln is in front of the restaurant. The ladies request they all sit in the back seat together to share some recipes. No problem, the men agree, and everyone piles into the car.

As they cross the Lincoln Memorial Bridge, Mims raises a question. "Do you think that restaurant is going to go under?" she asks.

"Why do you ask that?" inquires Swabbie.

"Well," Mims continues, "that time Anne wanted to borrow one of the picks used for the lobster dinner you made a big fuss, like it would have put them under if that pick disappeared."

"I didn't say it would put them under," exclaims Swabbie.

"Good," replies Mims. "Here, Anne, you can have this pick I borrowed. Swabbie said it won't put the restaurant under."

"I guess that means you can keep this pick, too," offers Jessie as she hands a second pick to Anne.

"Thank you both," responds Anne, "they will go nicely with the claw cracker." She goes into her purse and produces an almost-new cracker from the restaurant.

As the ladies are having a good chuckle in the back seat, Swabbie is on the attack.

"You had to get them started, didn't you, Jar Head? And what happened to, 'Don't worry, we'll watch them, Swabbie'? My special pair of agents. You can't even keep up with three women at a dinner table."

"Doesn't it give you a warm, secure feeling when you go to sleep at night, knowing these two are on the front lines of our national security?" Mims says.

"Yes, it does," answers Jessie. "How does that phrase go? 'Sleep well tonight, two of your front line national security agents usually are.'"

"You had to get them started," Swabbie grumbles again.

"Why do you keep blaming me?" asks Jar Head.

"They got us drunk-and besides, I think it was that 'You can say that again, look at my date' line from Doggie that got it all started."

"What about that?" yells Jessie from the back seat. "So much for the warriors' homecoming."

"You prick," Doggie whispers to Jar Head before he tries to talk himself out of this one.

Before they head home for coffee the group stops at the Top of the Town, where the two scientists, Jar Head and Doggie, conduct experiments on which gets more vodka, a gimlet straight up or a gimlet on the rocks. With the experiments completed, all decide to leave. When the elevator starts down, Doggie and Jar Head point behind Anne and yell, "Look out!", and when Anne turns she is looking through a glass wall at the rear of the elevator and a ten-story drop to the sidewalk.

After a scream, laughter and some foul language, everyone is again outside and climbing back into the car.

The Lincoln navigates through the Virginia countryside, and the discussion about the restaurant continues. Swabbie even asks if he can change sides and join the ladies' team.

It's good to be back home again with friends and lovers.

CHAPTER TWO

I t is 7 a.m. Doggie and Jar Head are in Swabbie's office piecing together all of the events leading up to, and including, their last operation.

Somewhere, there may be a piece of information that could throw some light on who set them up, or why.

While the Dynamic Duo are going through this process, Swabbie is attending a meeting about that same operation in the office of the Deputy Director of Operations (DDO). In attendance are the usual round up of intelligence analysts and the DDO's immediate subordinate, that certain Army general who keeps pushing to replace Jar Head and Doggie.

Swabbie has just completed his briefing on the operation, and is starting to address how the enemy troops could have known the team was going to be there.

"I can't believe those troops just happened to be camping out on the beach that night," Swabbie offers.

"Maybe it was just a patrol that stumbled onto them," asserts General Wallace.

"They haven't had night patrols on that island for years, because there isn't anything that important to guard," Swabbie retorts.

"Maybe they are getting too old and careless, and just brought attention to themselves," counters the general.

"Back to that again, are you?" snaps Swabbie.

"Well, answer this, big shot: how did the enemy patrol know to yell 'kill the Yankee dogs' when the attack started?"

At that remark, the general's face starts to get red as his anger rises.

"You don't know firsthand they said that," the general fires back "You just have the word of those two relics."

"Are you calling my men liars?" Swabbie says in a voice that everyone knows means business.

The two men nearly come to blows before a voice defuses the situation.

"Settle down, settle down," the DDO orders.

"General, I think we can accept the word of these two field operatives on this matter."

The general doesn't even acknowledge the DDO's words as he settles back into his seat.

The DDO continues with, "I think we will reschedule this meeting for a later date."

All agree and start to file out of the DDO's office when he says, "General can I have a moment?"

The general returns to his seat, and the others leave the office.

Swabbie has been back in his office for twenty minutes, and he's still pissed off about the meeting.

"Who does that Army prick think he is?" Swabbie rages.

Doggie and Jar Head are trying to calm him down before he says something really bad to the wrong person. Swabbie is just starting to settle down when Gert's voice comes over the intercom,

"Gil Dunn is coming this way," she informs her boss.

"Thanks, Gert,"

"Hi, Gert; how are things going?" Dunn asks the secretary.

"Pretty good, Gil. How about yourself?"

"Can't complain," answers Dunn as he continues toward the office door.

When the DDO enters the room, Jar Head and Doggie stand up and greet him. He, too, used to be in Field OPS. Greetings completed, they all sit to discuss the situation.

"Here's the scoop," Gil begins. "I put the general in his place, but you can bet he is already crying to his political contacts. I agree with you about the mission being compromised, but we have to come up with a reason why. It could be a vendetta against you two men, or someone may have a political agenda that is just taking off. Whatever it is, I will find out," he assures them.

The three men know Dunn very well, and understand that he doesn't talk just to hear himself talk.

"As we all know, one of the general's main objectives is to get you two replaced with two men of his own choosing." Dunn continues, "That shit is not going to happen, but in case I am overruled, I would like to have two men of your choosing." He motions towards Jar Head and Doggie.

"For the next week or so, I think it would be better if Swabbie was out of town," Dunn advises. "I have a feeling the general will be touching base with his high-powered political friends, especially after today's meeting, and they may go headhunting for Swabbie. If he goes too far in revealing classified information to reach his goal, I'll have him by the ass, and hopefully his friends as well."

The other three acknowledge the DDO's statements.

"Why don't you two take Swabbie on a week-long fishing trip or something?" inquires Dunn, "and at the same time, you can plan how you will go about selecting replacements, if needed."

"Sounds good to me," answers Doggie, with Jar Head in agreement.

"Okay, then. I'll see you three in about a week," Dunn says as he stands and moves to the door.

As Dunn turns the door knob, he adds, "You two try to get Swabbie into better shape, will you? Right now I think the general can take him, and it will be very embarrassing for me personally if the general kicks his ass at the next meeting."

That said, Dunn quickly opens the door and departs with a big smile on his face. Gert, who doesn't miss anything, joins Gil in a little chuckle as he passes her desk, when they hear a loud voice coming from Swabbie's office.

Fortunately, the only words they can make out are *General* and *dickhead*.

***

It is 6 a.m. when Swabbie kisses Anne and says goodbye to Mims and Jessie, who stopped over to have morning coffee with Anne. He then walks down the front steps of his house, grumbling that he doesn't like fishing, and *really* doesn't like running from a fight.

Doggie and Jar Head are waiting next to a station wagon that they somehow checked out of the Agency motor pool.

"What are you bitching about now?" asks Jar Head.

"Well, do you like fishing?" inquires Swabbie.

"No," answers Jar Head, "I prefer 'or something.'"

"You remember," Doggie offers, "Dunn said 'a fishing trip *or something.*'"

"What do you have in mind?"

"During the day, we're taking tours of historic military grounds, starting with Gettysburg."

"And nights are party time," adds Jar Head.

"Oh, that's different," approves Swabbie as he turns towards the house and waves goodbye to Anne.

"We'll take good care of him, Anne," Doggie reassures her.

"You better had," Anne warns, "and…"

"We know, we know," Jar Head interrupts her. "And there isn't a hole deep enough on Earth for us to hide in if anything does happens to him."

"And don't forget it," Anne confirms. She doesn't think twice about busting on Doggie or Jar Head, but she loves them both like brothers.

After the station wagon pulls out of the driveway and everyone has finished waving goodbye, Jar Head starts laughing.

"Are you thinking the same thing I am? Doggie asks.

"You better had...there isn't a hole deep enough on Earth?" replies Jar Head.

"She used to say that every time we went on a project," Doggie says.

"That's why you never got hurt," Jar Head tells Swabbie. "We would rather hit the enemy head-on to protect you than come back and face Anne."

The station wagon erupts into laughter as it proceeds down the road on the way to its first stop: Gettysburg.

It is mid-afternoon, and the three men are walking around Little Round Top at the Gettysburg Battlefield. After viewing the area overlooking 'devil's den,' where union snipers took a terrible toll on the confederate soldiers below, the three move on to visit the left flank of the Union lines and the place where Colonel Chamberlain led a bayonet charge, after his troops ran out of ammunition, that won the battle at Little Round Top and earned him the Medal of Honor. The three men are in a serious and respectful mood as they view and share information about the battles at Gettysburg.

This is especially true at the site of Picket's charge.

"My God!" exclaims Swabbie as he reads a plaque next to a battery of field cannons: "These cannons fired triple canisters point-blank at charging enemy troops. I can't even imagine something like that. Think about a 12-gauge shotgun blast, then try to figure how many hundreds of times you would have to multiply it to get close to the blast that came from these cannons that day."

Doggie shakes his head in agreement and the two men move on to join Jar Head, who is standing at the fence in front of the Union position. He scans the field in front of the Union lines as the other two arrive.

"I wonder what Lee was thinking about those three days?" he says aloud. "He was a great tactician, before and after the battles at Gettysburg. If he had listened to Longstreet, the Union would have been in pursuit of the confederate troops and they would have had their pick of defensive positions."

"He must have been convinced his troops could split the Union line in the middle; then the Union troops would retreat in disarray, and his boys would take the day and the battle?" offers Doggie.

"A terrible waste of men," offers Swabbie as he turns and walks back towards the car, followed by the other two.

Leaving the battlefield and returning to the town of Gettysburg, the three stop at one of the museums and are very interested in the display concerning the snipers of that age.

"Those snipers were reaching out there and touching folks," offers Jar Head.

"That many hundreds of yards is a surprising distance for the 1800's," agrees Doggie.

The trio continues their tour, and after checking out all of the bullet holes in the wall of a local restaurant, they adjourn to the bar.

"What do you think was the deciding factor in this battle?" inquires Swabbie.

"I think it was General Beaufort and his cavalry, who allowed the Union troops to get the high ground," offers Jar Head.

"I disagree," challenges Doggie, "I feel it was Chamberlain's charge. If the Confederate troops had gotten through his line, they would have been behind the Union lines."

"You're both wrong," corrects Swabbie. "It was the way General Lee called the shots."

That sounded the bell for round one and a long night's discussion. They plan to continue their tour the next day with a visit to Valley Forge, then move on to the place where Washington and his troops crossed the Delaware River, and into New Jersey.

***

The second day of the tour gets off to a later start…no need to get up and out while the fish are still biting.

After breakfast and another drive around the Gettysburg battlefield, the trio head for Harrisburg and the Pennsylvania turnpike. After driving on the turnpike for about an hour, the station wagon approaches the Valley Forge exit.

The first stop is the museum, followed by a visit to the defense positions and the troops' living quarters.

After lunch and stops at other places in the campgrounds, the men decide to move on to their next destination, Washington's Crossing. Wanting to see the countryside at a slower pace, they decide to follow Route 202 through Pennsylvania and into New Jersey. As they leave the Valley Forge area, Swabbie breaks the silence with a question.

"Have you two given any thought concerning Dunn's suggestion about training two replacements?"

"Yes, we're both kicking it around," answers Doggie.

"How do you feel about it?" inquires Swabbie.

"Our first thought was, 'Screw them'," answers Jar Head. "But then Doggie and I talked it over and decided it wasn't such a bad idea. We can't keep doing this forever-and who knows; our next mission may be our last."

"We also considered the fact that we would be doing the selecting and training," Doggie adds. "We will probably start deciding who we will try to recruit and how we will proceed today or tomorrow."

"Oh, by the way," Jar Head informs Swabbie, "If anyone asks, we are writers doing research for a book about two men back in 1776 that were selected for special duty during the Revolutionary War."

"Well, that's quaint," Swabbie says. "I suppose we'll use that as an explanation if anyone overhears your conversations."

"He's quick, isn't he?" Jar Head asks Doggie.

"Yes he is," confirms Doggie. "And I thought that in-house pussy job had slowed him down."

"In-house pussy job! If it wasn't for me, you two old goats would be in rocking chairs at the home."

These brief skirmishes continue off and on until the station wagon passes through one of the very small towns along Route 202.

"Let's check this out," Swabbie suggests as they approach a big sign that reads *Peddlers Village.* The other two agree, and they turn in and find a parking area.

After visiting the shops and buying gifts for their ladies, they decide to have dinner at the Cock & Bull restaurant. After a big meal that includes Swabbie practicing his elbow-bending technique, the three return to the wagon to continue their journey. Once in the car, Jar Head inquires, "What is it, Swabbie? The general?"

"How could you tell?" asks Swabbie.

"The elbow bending," answers Doggie.

"It bothers me when I see where things are heading," Swabbie explains. "It used to be us against this country's enemies. Now it seems to be that in addition to watching out for some of the people on our side and their secret agendas."

"Don't let it get to you," assures Doggie. "There is more good than bad at the Agency."

"That's true," Swabbie says, "but a few in high places can do a lot of damage, and Dunn is probably one of the few with the balls to fight them."

"Don't worry about the general," Jar Head reassures Swabbie. "If things get really rough, we'll just ask Anne to have a chat with him."

"Yes, we do have her as our secret weapon," answers Swabbie as he laughs and changes his position in the back seat.

"What the hell is this?" Swabbie complains as he tries to find out what is poking him. A search of the back seat produces a toy dart gun, with a rubber-tipped dart inserted and ready to fire.

"Where in the hell did this come from?"

"They must have used this wagon to move a family to another safe house," explains Doggie. "When I picked it up, they told me they hadn't had time to clean it out."

"What else is in here?" Swabbie wonders as he searches the back seat.

Doggie is about to pull out of Peddlers Village and back on to Route 202 when a rubber-tipped dart flies past his ear and sticks to the rearview mirror.

"What the fuck!" exclaims Doggie as he jumps in surprise. "You asshole, you almost gave me a heart attack," he says as he removes the dart.

It's hard to determine who's laughing harder, Swabbie or Jar Head-and it isn't long before Doggie joins them. The serious mood is broken, and they drive toward Washington's Crossing.

Twenty minutes later, the station wagon is stopped at a red light in Pettyville, New Jersey, and Swabbie is requesting that the back window of the station wagon be put down for ventilation.

Doggie grants his request, and the back window comes sliding down. As Swabbie turns to watch the window retract, he notices a police officer on a very small motorcycle behind them.

Swabbie waves to the officer on the bike, who ignores the friendly gesture...so Swabbie makes another gesture.

"Oh, this is good," comments Doggie as he catches what just happened in the rear view mirror.

The officer motions for the wagon to pull over, and Doggie complies.

Doggie is talking a mile a minute to the officer in an effort to calm the situation. Just when he is making headway, a rubber-tipped dart comes sailing out of nowhere and adheres to the side of the officer's helmet. Immediately, all eyes turn to the back seat to see Swabbie blowing imaginary smoke from the barrel of the dart gun.

Thirty minutes later, after surrendering the toy gun, the officer is still writing tickets...including, but not limited to, not wearing seat belts.

During their unplanned rest stop, the trio are looking around the area.

"That looks like a nice place to stay for the night," Jar Head says as he points across the street to the 'Pettyville House'.

"Take a walk over and see if they have any vacancies," suggests Doggie, "I'll be waiting here, because of you-know-who."

Ten minutes later, Jar Head returns to the wagon.

"I could only get two rooms, so Dart Man will have to sleep in the car," reports Jar Head with a smile.

When the officer finally finishes, he hands Doggie a hand full of tickets and returns to his bike.

"Can't they afford a man-sized bike in this town?" inquires Swabbie.

"I think we should call Anne," Jar Head says.

"You can call your granny, too, if you want," announces Swabbie.

After getting settled in their rooms, Doggie and Jar Head meet to discuss the selection process for the two new men they will be training. Swabbie is sitting on the second-floor porch that runs the entire length of the hotel, enjoying a cigar, when a group of motorcycle riders roars down the street and parks in front of the Pettyville House. The riders are wearing a wide assortment of helmets, including a replica of a German helmet from WWII.

As they are all in the process of turning off their engines and putting down the kickstands on their bikes, a rubber-tipped dart flies through the air and sticks to one of the German helmets. The biker removes his helmet to see what just hit it, and then says something to the man next to him. Shortly after the other man replies, the biker with the German helmet produces a Super Soaker water gun and sprays the laughing man on the second-floor porch. The man disappears from view as the bikers get a good laugh over it all.

Doggie and Jar Head are in the middle of a conversation when Swabbie rushes in asking if anyone has any rubbers with them. When the two say no, Swabbie makes a quick trip to the downstairs restroom, comes back up, and disappears into the bathroom. Jar Head is still looking at Doggie with a puzzled expression and is about to say something when Swabbie reappears with two water-filled rubbers and heads for the porch.

"What now?" Jar Head remarks.

"I hope it doesn't involve that policeman on the motorcycle," Doggie sighs.

Back on the porch, Swabbie takes aim at the German helmet with the first rubber, and has a near miss. The second rubber is overfull, and when Swabbie attempts to launch, it breaks and showers the entire group. Under a hail of debris and bad words, Swabbie disappears from view.

All of this commotion has grabbed the attention of a police officer, who has just come off duty and is on his way home. The officer parks his small bike next to the others, and is inquiring as to what all the commotion is about when he detects a slight thud on his helmet. Having previously felt a similar sensation, and taking his cue from the look on the bikers' faces, he says, "There's a dart stuck to my helmet, isn't there?"

The bikers confirm the officer's suspicion.

"Where?" the officer inquires.

One biker points to the second floor.

When the police officer looks at the second floor porch Swabbie holds up a toy dart gun and says, "I found two in the wagon." He then erupts in laughter.

Swabbie is in the middle of his second outburst when the officer produces a gun, aims and fires. A rubber-tipped dart sticks to the middle of Swabbie's forehead, interrupting his amusement. Swabbie looks cross-eyed as he tries to see what is stuck to his forehead. He reaches up, removes the dart, then looks down at the group.

The police officer smiles and blows imaginary smoke from the barrel of the first dart gun.

Swabbie again starts to laugh, and announces, "The drinks are on me. Everybody to the bar!"

Everyone in the group is in favor of that, and they all head inside. Swabbie stops to inform Doggie and Jar Head they are invited to a party downstairs, then continues his journey. Two hours later, the bikers, the police officer, Swabbie and his two friends are all enjoying themselves at the bar.

"Can I ask you something?" Swabbie says to the police officer.

"Sure," the officer replies.

"How come you have such a small bike?"

"Well, it goes like this," the officer says. "They want me to retire because of my age, and are trying everything they can to get their way. This bike is the latest attempt. It's small, and it makes me look stupid, but that's just as well because I didn't know how to ride one, and I think a big bike would have been too much for me." Swabbie agrees with the officer that it's unfair, and continues talking with him for the rest of the evening.

The next morning, Swabbie is at the front desk asking for directions. One hour later, the wagon pulls into a Harley dealership in Pennsylvania. Already waiting in the parking lot is the biker with the German helmet. Doggie, Jar Head and Swabbie don't know anything about buying a Harley Sporter, so they brought along their new friend. Besides, somebody has to show the officer how to ride the new big bike he doesn't know he's getting.

After paying for the Harley and putting it in the police officer's name, they force the biker to accept money for the instructions he'll be giving the officer on how to handle the bike. Having financed and recruited personnel for this clandestine operation, they thank the biker and bid him farewell and good luck before they head once again for Washington's Crossing.

CHAPTER THREE

O ne week has passed, and Swabbie is back at work. He's had two additional PCs hooked up and placed on the small conference table in his office, and Jar Head and Doggie are busy accessing personnel files in an effort to find their new trainees.

Doggie is focusing on the Army Special Forces and Rangers, while Jar Head is onto the Navy Seals, Marine Corps Force recon and the Scout/Sniper files.

This routine lasts for ten days before both men make their selections. That completed, Doggie and Jar Head swap all of the information regarding their choices with each other for review, and one day later they are ready to submit their selections to Swabbie.

The following morning, the three are seated in Swabbie's office ready for review.

"How many candidates do we have?" inquires Swabbie.

"Two," replies Doggie.

"Two each, I hope," Swabbie says.

"Why?" Jar Head asks. "Do you think it will take four men to replace us?"

"You know what I mean," snaps Swabbie. "You haven't even seen these people in person yet, and you've decided on just two?"

"I told you he was sharp," Jar Head says to Doggie.

"Let me guess," Swabbie continues. "One is in the Army and one is in the Marine Corps?"

"This is getting scary now," Doggie observes. "He seems to be developing special skills that enable him to see into the future."

"That, or he's eating Gypsy shit again," Jar Head adds.

"Okay, you old farts, let's see what you got," Swabbie orders. "You first, Doggie."

"My selection is currently an enlisted man, a sergeant in the Army Special Forces (Green Berets). He's been through Airborne Jump School and Ranger training, so that makes him an Airborne Ranger as well. As you can see, he seems to have a natural tendency towards special OPS-type units, and has the ability to make the grade in all of these units.

"Those are the highlights, and you can read through this file I have prepared for any additional info," says Doggie as he hands a folder to Swabbie.

"My selection is also an enlisted man and a sergeant, but is a Marine Corps Scout/Sniper. Prior to that, he was in Force Recon, went through Jump School and wears the same parachute jump wings as the other man. Like Doggie's selection, this man seems to have a natural tendency towards special OPS units, and my guess is his next request will be for Seals training.

"I have also prepared a file you can review," says Jar Head as he hands his folder to Swabbie.

"I guess your next step is to visit with these men in person?" asks Swabbie.

"Our plan," offers Doggie, "is to first observe them. After that, we will make contact."

"Will the arrangements for personal contacts be made through you or the DDO?" asks Jar Head.

"If you like what you see after you observe your selections, get in touch with me and I will make the arrangements for a personal interview. We work with the military, especially with these types of units, and if we want to speak with one of their people we put in a request."

"I guess that means we fly tomorrow," Doggie says, "first to Fort Campbell, Kentucky, then on to Camp Lejeune, North Carolina."

"Since these two men will be doing very special ops, I think we should conceal their true identity from the start," Swabbie instructs. "Have you come up with anything in that area?"

"No," replies Doggie. "We figure we'll know it when we see it."

"Since you have been out of the field for a few weeks, I thought it would be a good idea for you to go through a little drill to get you back up to speed," Swabbie informs the other two. "We're going to Harvey's tonight to see if you two old farts can keep track of the movements of three ladies at a dinner table."

"Oh, that's funny," replies Jar Head.

"I think it's a good idea," approves Doggie. "After dessert, we can tell the ladies about the continuing adventures of 'DART MAN!'"

The room erupts into laughter, and the three reflect on their week-long tour.

***

Three weeks, later the initial observations and all of the interviews have been completed. Doggie and Jar Head decide it's time to see how the new selections interact in a public place. During the interviews, both Jar Head and Doggie picked up on an extreme sense of pride in both of their selections. Both men take pride in the units they belong to, and themselves. They were not hostile towards each other, but it probably wouldn't take much to set them off. For this reason, Doggie and Jar Head select a place in rural Maryland in case things get unpleasant.

Officially, both selections are still on active duty and are wearing their class 'A' uniforms. The changeover to summer uniforms hasn't occurred yet, so Marine Corps greens and Special Forces winter uniform, complete with green beret, are in order.

The car containing the four men proceeds around the Washington D.C. beltway and exits onto Indian Head Highway. Several miles down this road the population starts to thin out. After driving a few more miles, the four-door sedan pulls off the road and into the parking lot of a restaurant. After the car is parked in front of the building, the four men get out and proceed to the front door. Upon entering, all four men check out the clientele. They look like a rough bunch of locals, but nothing serious.

They proceed to a table, and Jar Head volunteers to get the first round. After two rounds have been consumed, the new recruits start to loosen up, and a little Army - Marine Corps jousting begins. Jar Head and Doggie knew this was going to happen sooner or later, but don't know how serious it will get. Things don't seem to be getting too serious, and Doggie and Jar Head are relieved.

Things are going along pretty well when the Marine inquires about a rest room. The downstairs is out of order, so he has to climb the stairs to use the second-floor facilities. A few minutes later, the Army man volunteers to get the next round. After placing his order at the bar, he waits for the drinks. A bit of laughter erupts from the men sitting at the bar, but he ignores it. A few seconds later the man sitting on the stool next to him says, "Pretty hat." Still, the man is ignored. Again the man addresses the Army sergeant: "Is that a green tam?" and again, he is ignored. The man on the stool gets a little mad.

"Hey, I'm asking you about that quaint little beanie, and I don't like being ignored," the man insists.

"I don't care," replies the Green Beret as he looks at the man eye-to-eye.

"I don't think you people are so bad," offers the man.

"I don't care about that either."

With that, the man takes a cheap shot with his left hand. The Green Beret steps to the rear with his left foot, uses his left hand to block and pull the man's left arm so that he flies off the stool, and nails him with a right hand as he passes in front of him. The attacker is out cold when he hits the floor.

His pals at the bar don't like what just happened, and all of them jump on the Green Beret. Doggie and Jar Head are in the process of standing up to assist when the Marine comes running down the stairs, dives over the banister and into the group of men fighting.

"Holy shit," exclaims Jar Head.

With the new entry into the fray, the locals lose interest in the fight and revert to talking.

After paying their bill, the four return to their car and head down Indian Head highway towards Washington.

"I haven't seen anything like that since I watched a blue jay dive straight into a bunch of starlings," Jar Head observes.

"It's what I do," replies the Marine.

"Now let me get this straight," starts Doggie.

"You punch out one man, are attacked by his friends, then the other one dives off the staircase like a big-ass bird and into the bunch, all because they made fun of your green beanie?"

"Something like that."

Doggie looks at Jar Head, who is riding in the front passenger seat, and says, "Well I guess that answers that question."

Then both men announce at the same time, "Blue Jay and Bean," and start to laugh.

In the back seat, Blue Jay and Bean smile and ask each other how they wound up with these two people.

***

The morning following the restaurant incident, Doggie and Jar Head are sitting in the section chief's office with the men they have selected as their eventual replacements. Swabbie has just finished an informal interview with the two when Gert comes over the intercom.

"Gil Dunn is heading this way."

"Thanks, Gert," Swabbie replies after pressing a button on his intercom, then announces, "It looks like you're about to meet the DDO. But don't worry, he's good people."

Just then the door opens, and Gil Dunn walks in.

"Gil, I would like you to meet the selections for the two positions you told us to recruit for."

As everyone stands, Swabbie starts the introductions. "This man was selected by Doggie, and his code name is Bean." Bean extends his hand and gives Mr. Dunn a firm handshake. After a few words of welcome, Gil looks at the other man.

"And this man is Jar Head's selection," Swabbie continues, "code name Blue Jay."

Dunn can see this man is not really impressed with all of this and decides to have a little fun with him.

"Blue Jay," Dunn repeats as he shakes his hand. "They like to get into fights, don't they?"

"Yes, sir," confirms Jar Head.

"Well, I hope that is the case here, and he doesn't turn out to be just another pretty blue bird."

Blue Jay and Dunn are still shaking hands and looking each other straight in the eye while the others hold their breath, waiting for the next word to be spoken. After a pause, Blue Jay says,"Gil…if that is part of your code name, did someone have a fish in mind?"

"A shark, to be exact," replies Dunn.

"Oh, I see," acknowledges Blue Jay, pretending they are having a serious conversation.

Seeing this might be a good time to cut in, Swabbie says, "I just finished an informal interview and was about to get into the details, if these men are still interested. Would you like to sit in?" Swabbie inquires.

Dunn looks at his watch and surprises everyone when he says, "Yes, I would; we may as well let them know what they are in for at all levels if they decide to come aboard."

One hour into the briefing, Dunn's beeper goes off and he quickly checks the message as it rolls across the display.

"Sorry, it looks like I have to go," Dunn announces, then turns to the two new men and asks, "Do you think you'd be interested?"

Bean and Blue Jay respond at the same time with positive answers.

"Good," Dunn says, and shakes hands with both men before leaving.

Once Dunn is out of the office Jar Head starts to reflect. "Oh, that went well. Now, what did my selection say again? Could it have been 'part of a fish?' "

"Yeah," laughs Doggie, "that message on his beeper probably told him your room was ready at the retirement village."

"Don't worry about it," Swabbie reassures everyone. "Dunn was looking for a reaction, and Blue Jay didn't disappoint him."

"Whatever," comments Blue Jay as everyone turns to look at him.

"Oh, yeah. I can see this kid is going to get me sent to the village," Jar Head exclaims.

CHAPTER FOUR

S ince Blue Jay and Bean are on active duty with the military, and already expert in several areas, no training will be required for weapons, hand-to-hand combat and the like. Instead, the training will be more like grad school, with Jar Head and Doggie acting as professors. The two professors will share with their new students things they have learned over the years...having been active in field OPS for so long, they must be doing something right.

Doggie and Jar Head decide to set up school in northeast Pennsylvania. For training purposes, this will put them within commuting distance to large cities like Philadelphia and New York City, and at the same time be close to some of the rural areas of Pennsylvania. For ocean and beach tactics, the Jersey shore is only 80 miles away.

It is 1:30 PM when a burgundy van pulls onto what looks like a small dirt road that goes nowhere. The road continues for about a quarter of a mile, with a field on one side and a wooded area on the other. It then turns to the left and disappears into the woods. Fifty yards later, the van stops in front of a large cabin-type residence sometimes used by the Agency as a safehouse. Having a structure tucked away in the woods in this part of Pennsylvania is nothing out of the ordinary. Celebrities and wealthy people have maintained this type of residence for years, and use them for a weekend getaway or a second country home outside of New York City or Philadelphia.

The four men get out and start to unpack the van: personal luggage first, then additional gear that Doggie and Jar Head have brought along for training purposes. The cabin is always kept well-stocked with food, and when it is going to be used a staff arrives the day before and readies everything for its new arrivals. There are four bedrooms upstairs for the guests, and two downstairs usually used for security and house staff, but no additional staff will be required for this visit. Jar Head and Doggie have set up a schedule that gives them the first two days to get more acquainted with their new recruits, and then they will follow a schedule of classroom-type training to share some of the things they have picked up over the years-and to test

Bean and Blue Jay on their ability to pick up and make suggestions for improving the tactics. Since the new recruits are well experienced in the field, urban tactics will be the first thing on the agenda. Philadelphia and NYC will be used as training areas. For training in the field, the forests will be used. When Doggie and Jar Head are satisfied with the progress of their new students, a series of tests will be developed to test student against teacher.

***

Two months have passed, and the teachers are very pleased with the progress of the students. During the urban portion of the training, Blue Jay has shown his ability to blend in and become almost invisible when running training exercises in the city. This ability has been noted, and will be further developed in the future.

The rural portion has taken much less time, and it isn't long before Doggie and Jar Head find themselves transformed from teachers to peers, sharing ideas with the other two men. They decide it's test time.

The first series of tests consist of Doggie and Jar Head tracking and locating the two students. The students' objectives are to evade…or ambush, if possible.

Two tests run over a three-day period put the score at students, one, and teachers, one. The fourth day is used to review the previous three days and prepare for the next round of tests, where Bean and Blue Jay will be the hunters. The fifth day, Jar Head and Doggie catch their students in an ambush, and the score goes to 2 to 1 in favor of the teachers.

The morning of day six has Doggie and Jar Head leaving the cabin area. They will be given a two-hour head start before being pursued. One hour into their flight, Doggie and Jar Head split up in opposite directions. Thirty minutes later, Doggie approaches railroad tracks that haven't been used in years. Walking on the rails and ties so he will not leave any tracks, he heads back towards the cabin area.

Jar Head has located a good-sized stream that runs through the forest, and is heading upstream. Ten minutes later he has left the water and is picking his way across the stony surface alongside the stream. When he runs out of rocks to step on, he jumps to the shore. After a few steps, he reaches up and takes hold of a low-hanging tree limb and swings himself back onto the rocky surface. That accomplished, he returns to the stream and heads back in the direction he just came from. With the current and the depth of the water, his tracks should not be detected.

This test will force the pursuers to split up, and then each man will have to make a guess on which way to continue the search.

Four hours pass, and both students are searching. Having left telltale signs that only a very good tracker would notice, Doggie and Jar Head have sent their students off in the wrong direction and returned to the cabin. After freshening up, the two teachers head out for some relaxed dining.

At 6 AM the following morning, the beepers Bean and Blue Jay are carrying start to vibrate. *Are you children lost?* scrolls across the screen, followed by *Everyone in.* When Blue Jay and Bean get back to the cabin, the teachers are sitting on the front porch enjoying a cup of coffee.

"Now, let me see," Doggie says, "that makes the score students, 1 and teachers…is it 3? Yes, I believe it's 3."

"Don't feel bad," encourages Jar Head. "Just try to remember, *'Keep cool in the pool and use your head'.*"

Both students know there is a third part to that saying: *'be observant'* but they don't want to correct the teacher.

While having something to eat, the two students request another chance on the following day. Later in the day they tell their teachers they are going for a long run to clear their heads, and that the training may have overwhelmed them a little and made them careless. After being reassured by their teachers that probably wasn't the case, the two depart for their run.

The following morning, after executing a tactic similar to the one they used the previous day, the teachers are walking up to the cabin.

"Where do you want to go for dinner?" asks Jar Head.

"How about that restaurant you, me and Dart Man went to during our tour?" offers Doggie.

"That sounds good," the other confirms.

The activity at the cabin has not gone unnoticed. A pair of field glasses has both men in focus as they enter the dwelling.

"I knew they were playing games with us," exclaims Blue Jay.

"Yeah, we were both on the beam on that one," agrees Bean.

"'Be cool in the pool,'" Blue Jay mocks. "Well, there's another saying in the Corps: *catch me, fuck me.* And we caught them."

A short time later, Jar Head and Doggie reappear and get into the van for the drive to the restaurant. Not knowing the destination of the two, Bean and Blue Jay follow at a distance on a motorcycle they rented the day before during their run.

The teachers order a fine dinner of beef Wellington, and are enjoying coffee and an after-dinner drink when the waiter approaches the table and announces, "I have a note for you two gentlemen." Doggie looks confused as he reaches out to retrieve the piece of paper. After opening the folded note he reads: *Be cool in the pool, use your head and try to be observant,* **Teach**. *Your transportation home is where the van was parked.*

When Jar Head and Doggie return to the parking lot, a Harley Hog motorcycle is parked where the van used to be. Another note is attached to the seat and reads: *We didn't want you both to get killed trying to ride this bike home, so we disabled it.* Call Towle Towing at this number. *Signed, the students xoxoxoxo'.*

"We must be getting old," laughs Doggie.

"Or we selected very well," Jar Head says as he joins his partner in laughter.

Two and one half hours pass, and a tow truck pulls up in front of the cabin. As Ed Towle is unloading the Harley from the Jerr-Dan, the students emerge from the cabin, each with a drink in one hand and a cigar in the other.

"We tried to tell them not to ride that bike," Blue Jay announces, "but you know how it goes. The fathers don't like to listen to their sons."

Ed smiles and shakes his head in agreement as Bean approaches him. The bill had already been taken care of, but Bean gives Mr Towle two additional twenty-dollar bills for his trouble and says, "You can't tell these old farts anything." Ed laughs and thanks everyone for being so generous, then departs.

"Well, that was fun," Doggie remarks.

"Not as much fun as wandering around in the woods all night," Bean retorts.

"These students have no respect for their teachers," exclaims Jar Head.

"That's not necessarily true," corrects Blue Jay, then after a brief pause adds, "Ya old fart."

Jar Head looks at Doggie, and both men start to laugh as Doggie announces, "School's out."

"Let's go in and start the graduation party," suggests Jar Head, and all head for the cabin.

CHAPTER FIVE

T he location for training has moved in-house at Langley, Virginia. Having been mostly in the field or living in barracks during their tours in the military, Bean and Blue Jay feel a little awkward as they walk down the halls at CIA headquarters, but they are both quick learners, and with Doggie and Jar Head as their mentors they feel at ease in short order.

The first order of business is a formal introduction to Gert. On their previous visit to Swabbie's office, it was a quick hello on the way in. As they approach Gert's desk she looks up, and immediately a big smile lights up her face.

"Gert," Jar Head announces, "I would like you to meet two new people..." but before Jar Head can continue with the introductions, Gert interrupts.

"Bean and Blue Jay, welcome aboard," she says and offers her hand to Bean, then Blue Jay.

"Is there anything you don't know?" inquires Jar Head.

"Not in this office," Gert replies with a smile.

"You'd think I would stop asking that question after this many years," Jar Head says.

"You would think," Gert confirms.

Bean and Blue Jay are amused by the exchange, and decide Gert is 'good people', like Jar Head and Doggie. Swabbie seems okay as well, but school is still out for Blue Jay when it comes to Gil Dunn.

After supplying Gert with information she requires concerning the new people, the four men go into Swabbie's office.

"I see you are still with us?" Swabbie observes as the men enter the room.

"Yes Sir," replies Doggie, "we tried to discourage them, but they insisted on staying."

The four men smile at Doggie's statement as they all take seats in front of Swabbie's desk.

"You men are at a point in your training where you can either turn down this opportunity and return to your military units, or you can stay on board and go into the next phase. Can we assume you are in, or would you like to go back to your units?"

Blue Jay and Bean look at each other, and then confirm by saying, "We're in."

"Good," Swabbie says. "From here on, we will be getting into highly classified information, and of course, the politics of Washington, D.C.

"I have been going over both of your backgrounds, and I have a few questions," Swabbie continues. "Bean, your serving with Special Forces speaks for itself, but I notice you also speak a half-dozen languages from the old Soviet block countries."

"Yes, sir," Bean confirms, "learning new languages seems to be easy for me."

"Good," Swabbie replies. "The cold war may be over, but there are still a lot of things going on in that part of the world.

"Blue Jay, your tours in the Corps seem to go from Japan to Scout/Sniper, then Japan and back again."

"Yes, sir," Blue Jay says. "I have been fortunate in my assignments."

"We know what you bring to the table from the Scout/Sniper assignments," Swabbie acknowledges.

"Do you have any additional skills that you acquired during your tours in Japan?"

"Yes, sir. I studied martial arts during both tours."

"Which of them did you study? "Swabbie inquires.

"The usual, plus Ninjitsu," replies Blue Jay. "It is a martial art modeled after the Ninja clans that served the War Lords of Japan."

"During your Ninjutsu training, did you specialize in any one area?"

"Yes, sir...movement and concealment."

"Don't you cover that in your Scout/Sniper school?" Jar Head inquires.

"Yes sir, but the training in Japan covered both city and in the field, not just in the field."

"Good, good," approves Swabbie, already thinking of how he can put Blue Jay's skills to good use.

Swabbie then turns his attention to Jar Head and Doggie. "How did the training sessions in Pennsylvania go?"

"Very well," answers Doggie. "I think we have made two good selections."

"They both seem to have MOs similar to Doggie and myself," adds Jar Head. "It's almost like we are their FATHERS!" Jar Head continues, referring to the motorcycle episode in Pennsylvania.

"Now that you mention that, it does seem that way," confirms

Doggie as both men look at their new trainees.. Blue Jay and Bean just shrug their shoulders and act like they don't know what they are referring to.

Swabbie takes this all in, and surmises the younger two got the better of their teachers in Pennsylvania.

He also knows if they did, Doggie and Jar Head will enjoy telling him about it during off-hours. Between the facts and their storytelling abilities, it should be a lot of laughs.

Swabbie once again takes charge of the meeting.

"For the next week, we'll get the men familiar with the headquarters building, introduce them to the departments they will be interfacing with, and brief them on some of the current operations. I think the four of you should plan and execute a minor operation. If the general gets enough clout to override the DDO, we may have to make the change very quickly to keep him from getting his two selections in place, and I don't what Bean and Blue Jay to be thrown into a dangerous situation without being prepared."

The four men agree with Swabbie's words and continue the meeting, expressing their ideas and concerns. Two hours later, the meeting is adjourned and the four men leave Swabbie's office to start their tour of the building.

***

The following morning, Doggie and Jar Head are continuing the tour started the day before when they pass an Army colonel in the hallway.

"Morning," Doggie and Jar Head mutter as they keep walking past the man. Once out of earshot, Jar Head announces, "That's Colonel Monet, one of the general's flunkies."

"An asswipe if there ever was one," adds Doggie.

"We'll give you a complete rundown on the good
 people and the jerks tomorrow," Jar Head continues, "but for now we'll navigate around the jerks." Blue Jay and Bean acknowledge, and the tour continues.

Two hours pass, and the tour has left the headquarters building and is now in downtown Washington, D.C.

"When we are planning an operation," Doggie starts, "we try to touch base with these folks to get a better idea about what we are up against, and a look at the terrain in the area where the operation will take place. They usually have the information we are looking for at NPIC (National Photographic Interruption Center). It gives us access to a wealth of current and historical information. If they don't have what we need and the operation has a high level of importance, they can make arrangements to get the required information."

It is late afternoon as the four men are leaving NPIC, and Jar Head suggests a trip to Harvey's for an early dinner. After navigating through rush hour traffic the four are at the restaurant and surrendering the car to valet parking. Once inside, they are seated at their usual table, order drinks and start to talk about things in general. It is early, and they are the only patrons seated for dinner.

After some small talk and checking out the area for big ears, Jar Head asks in a low voice, "Are you men still in?"

"Without a doubt," Bean answers.

"What about you?" Doggie asks Blue Jay.

"Of course," answers Blue Jay, still looking at his glass in deep thought.

"Good show," announces Jar Head as he raises his glass in a toast.

After clicking glasses and taking a sip of their drinks, the men again sit quietly.

"I know I'm going to regret asking this, but what are you thinking about, Blue Jay?" Jar Head inquires.

"What's the story on Gil Dunn?" Blue Jay asks without any hesitation.

"That little voice told me not to ask him what was on his mind," announces Jar Head, "but would I listen? Nooo."

"Look at it this way," Doggie informs Jar Head.

"It's just another little piece of information telling you that sooner or later the kid is going to piss off the DDO, and as punishment your ass will be sent to the retirement village."

"I know that," replies Jar Head, "but I'm in denial."

"Why do you say that?" Blue Jay inquires.

"Because we were watching you and Dunn in Swabbie's office that day, and we both know you will probably not back down if he pushes you a little."

"That's why I'm asking," Blue Jay informs everyone. "If he is good people, it will be okay if he pushes. If he's an asshole it won't be okay."

Jar Head looks at Doggie, then stands up, raises his hand and announces to the waiter, "Two more rounds, please."

Doggie chuckles, then starts to answer Blue Jay's question. "First of all, Dunn is a good man. He's from the old school and calls it like it is. Sometimes that doesn't go over too well in today's Washington, but that hasn't changed the way he does things. He was a field operative in his younger days. Then, he and Swabbie decided to continue their careers in-house. You couldn't ask for better bosses, and they are both very good people."

"Now, as for you and Dunn," Jar Head takes over the

conversation, "Doggie and I both know that sooner or later you two will probably be butting heads for one reason or another, and that's okay. We've been joking about it, but that's all it is: joking. We are not worried about any repercussions from your actions. We never worried about the consequences of the things we did, so why should we worry about you?"

"That's for sure," adds Doggie. "Remember the time you pissed off the Deputy Director of Intelligence? I thought you were a goner for sure that time."

"Ah, don't bring that up," pleads Jar Head. "I'm trying to set a good example for the lads."

Doggie starts telling the story about Jar Head and the DDI as another round of drinks arrive. It will be the first of many stories told that night as the lads start to really get to know their newfound fathers.

***

The following morning, the four men are again meeting in Swabbie's office to discuss the training mission, or graduation exam, as Doggie and Jar Head like to call it.

"I may have found the ideal project for the training mission," announces Swabbie. "It's something that needs doing, but when compared to other projects, it doesn't have priority. With what we have in mind, though, it's ideal."

That said, Swabbie moves to the table in his office often used for this type of planning, and unfolds a map and other documents.

"As you can see, this is a map of Nassau in the Bahamas," Swabbie announces. "There is a group that makes its headquarters in the middle of Nassau, at a place we call The Pink Palace. They are a small group, but growing bolder and bolder with their exploits, and each time they pull something off, they get more members."

"We have heard about this group, but why did you select them?" Doggie inquires.

"For one reason: we want to hit them before they get any bigger. At present they may have some officials on their payroll, but nothing serious. We feel if someone takes out this group, the local authorities will take it as a sign of goodwill."

"Does take them out mean take them *all* out?" Jar Head asks.

"In this case, that will not be necessary," answers Swabbie. "The head man and his two top men will be enough. Right now this group has no cause to rally around. Just kidnapping, a little drug running; things like that. If we take out the top three people it should be enough."

"Any questions?" asks Swabbie.

Jar Head and Doggie shake their heads no.

"Okay then, that's it," confirms Swabbie, and the three men stand and start to walk away from the table. Blue Jay and Bean are still seated at the table, and look at the three men.

"That's it?" inquires Blue Jay.

"Oh, I'm sorry," apologizes Swabbie. "I am so used to this routine with these two, I neglected to ask if you had any questions."

"Is that all in the way of briefings?" asks Bean.

"No," replies Swabbie. "At this point Doggie and Jar Head will start preparing for the project by gathering information about the group, doing analysis and developing several plans for the project. When they are satisfied, we will meet again and, depending on what the project is, the DDO may sit in on our last meeting prior to executing the plan. Any other questions?"

"No, sir," both men answer. They get up and move to join the others.

"The DDO again," Blue Jay mumbles to Bean.

"Is this a problem with Gil Dunn, or just management in general?" asks Bean.

"Both," quips Blue Jay.

Jar Head and Doggie are walking ahead of the other two, but make it a point not to miss anything anyone says.

"Maybe I'll just take retirement now," Jar Head tells Doggie.

"And miss all of the fun?" asks Doggie. "You just know that sooner or later, Dunn and Blue Jay are going to have an event."

"That's true," Jar Head confirms. "Maybe I'll stick around.

Both men laugh as they head down the hall to start gathering intelligence data.

CHAPTER SIX

The Jamaica Air flight from Chicago has landed, and all passengers have collected their luggage, gone through the new arrivals routine at the airport, and are now outside the main entrance loading into cabs for the ride to their hotels. Blue Jay and Bean have a cab lined up for the ride to their hotel at Paradise Island, and are loading their luggage into the trunk. That completed, they get into the back seat and the cab starts its journey. As the cab is leaving the airport grounds, Blue Jay nudges Bean with his elbow and Bean starts talking about how beautiful everything is as he scans the area. When his vision reaches the extreme left he sees the reason for the nudge.

An American Airlines jet, recently arrived from Washington, D.C., is parked on the airport grounds and has started to offload its passengers. Halfway down the stairs are two distinguished-looking men already getting into the swing of things, and enjoying the start of their week-long vacation. Probably two teachers on holiday.

After descending the stairs, Doggie and Jar Head enter the terminal building and go through the same routine as their students did earlier. Once outside, they make arrangements for a cab to take them to a hotel at Cable Beach.

With them at Cable Beach and the students at Paradise Island, their objective, The Pink Palace, will be in the middle. Using different airlines from different locations in the U.S., and staying at hotels a good distance from each other, no one should connect the four men as being together. Doggie and Jar Head are already well known in Nassau by the criminal and other undesirable elements of the society, and are purposely drawing attention to themselves. Hopefully, this will assist their students in completing their final exam.

Jar Head and Doggie spend the remainder of the day and evening at Cable Beach, having a good time and drawing even more attention to themselves as Bean and Blue Jay perform recon at the Pink Palace. When evening approaches, the two men split up.

Bean explores the first floor, the grounds and beach outside in more detail, while Blue Jay does his specialty, getting in and out of places without being seen. Staying out of sight of the main desk, that always seem to know who are supposed to be guests and who are not, Blue Jay finds an unattended stairway and, acting like one of the hotel guests, ascends to the second floor. From here on it gets tricky, but between acting like a guest and doing his invisible act, Blue Jay works his way up to the higher floors of the hotel. This hotel is old, but some of the rooms are quite nice. Blue Jay finds this out during his journey, as several times he is forced to unlock and enter one of the guest rooms.

Within ten minutes, he is on the floor just below where their targets reside. After checking the rooms at each end of the hall and the balconies, Blue Jay returns to the second floor and the stairway he used earlier.

Once again, he has to act as though he has a legitimate reason for being there. Blue Jay stands at the end of the hall, looking out the window at the beach and at the same time watching the hallway behind him in the window's reflection. After about five minutes, he hears the latch on one of the guest room doors. Checking out the reflection, he sees a pretty redhead enter the far end of the hall, walking towards the stairway. Blue Jay reaches down and pulls the fly on his pants halfway down, then turns and walks towards the same stairs. Reaching the stairs at the same time as the redhead, Blue Jay, always the gentleman, motions for the lady to go first. The redhead smiles, and Blue Jay engages her in conversation about the beauty of the beach and the water as they come down the steps. When Blue Jay knows he is in camera range, he reaches down and pulls his fly back up, adjusts his pants and buttons his sport coat.

Between his actions and the redhead seeming pleased with their conversation, hotel security will assume romance was the reason this man was on the second floor. To keep this assumption going, and for his own enjoyment, Blue Jay asks the lady to dinner and spends a lovely night with a lovely lady.

Bean has a similar situation going on with a brunette at the hotel's beach area. Who said it has to be all work?

***

Meanwhile, Doggie and Jar Head are having a good time at Cable Beach. If they drew any more attention to themselves, they would probably get arrested.

Doggie looks at his watch and quips, "It's 10 p.m., do you know where your children are?"

"They'll be okay," Jar Head assures him. "They probably did their recon and went back to their hotel, like good little sergeants."

"Are you forgetting about the tow truck episode?" Doggie inquires.

"Now why did you have to bring that up?" asks Jar Head. "Now I'm going to be wondering about them until tomorrow night."

***

The next day is uneventful, with the exception of making contact with a local British intelligence agent to collect weapons and other goodies.

As evening approaches, outside lighting starts to come on around the Pink Palace. The terrace, the beach area, and especially the hotel's cabana bar, about 30 yards off the beach, come to life. It's an ideal place for a bar: sitting out on the water, with a sea breeze keeping the customers cool, while specialty drinks are consumed. It's a good money-maker for the hotel…and an even better place for a diversion.

Nightfall has arrived completely when two men walk into the Pink Palace's lobby and travel the width of the hotel to the beach. Once there, they locate the walkway to the cabana bar and continue their journey. By the time they reach the cabana and take two seats at the bar, the targets and their henchmen have been informed of their presence, and a team has been dispatched to keep an eye on them. Since their arrival yesterday, it has appeared they are on holiday, but with this type you never know.

As the night wears on, the two continue drinking at a normal pace, chatting with the other customers and buying an occasional round of drinks. After a few hours, it seems the two really are on vacation, and the team that was dispatched to watch them relax a little and relay their observations back to the boss from time to time.

Another hour passes and the watchers are still in place. Things at the hotel go back to normal.

Thirty minutes later, Blue Jay has once again made his way to the upper floors of the hotel and is in the process of checking out security. With a large group watching Doggie and Jar Head, security is a little light. Once Blue Jay is satisfied he has located all of the men on guard, he gives the silencer on his .22 Blackhawk a twist to make sure it's snug.

The stairway door is in the center of the hallway, and there are men on guard next to the door and at either end of the hall. Blue Jay looks at his watch, takes a deep breath and waits quietly for his opportunity. Five minutes later, the sound of pebbles hitting the glass on the balcony doors is heard at the end of the hall, where the leaders of the group all hold their suites of rooms. The man on guard looks out of the window, then reaches down, turns the knob on the door and moves onto the balcony. After checking out the balcony and the balconies on each side, he proceeds to the railing and looks over the edge to check the floor below. As he does, muffled sounds at ground level are heard and the guard falls to his left side, hit by two rounds from Bean's weapon.

The guard falls over a chair, causing a noise and a reason for the others to investigate. First, the guard by the hallway door leaves his post, with the man at the other end of the hall following. The first man reaches the balcony door and cautiously proceeds out to investigate. When the other guard passes the hallway door, Blue Jay moves quickly into the hallway with him and is closing the distance between them. Before the man realizes he is there, Blue Jay hits the man in the back of the head with his Blackhawk, and the guard goes down for the count.

At that same moment, the remaining guard on the balcony has started to sound the alarm. As Blue Jay continues down the hall, a door opens to his right. He recognizes the man in the doorway as one of the targets and disposes of him quickly.

After taking his first two shots, Bean moves further away from the hotel so he can have a better view of anyone on the balcony. Blue Jay continues toward the balcony door, and as he approaches it another door opens to his left to reveal the main target. At the same time, the guard on the balcony draws his weapon and takes aim. Blue Jay quickly fires two rounds into the head of the man in the doorway and turns to fire at the guard, but finds there is no need. Bean had the angle and took the shot, and the guard has fallen over a small table. As Blue Jay turns back to the open door, he catches sight of target number three as he slams the steel door shut.

Not getting through that door, he thinks, and goes out onto the balcony. Bean is already prepared, and when he sees Blue Jay he fires a small grappling hook and line to the opposite side of the balcony. With the hook in hand, Blue Jay goes back to the door and positions the hook so half of it is against the inside of the door and the other half is against the door frame, and pulls the door closed. This will be his anchor, and anyone trying to get out will be unable to cut the steel hooks to get the door open.

Blue Jay then proceeds to the edge of the balcony, climbs over the railing and rappels down to ground level. With one hand Bean holds the rope away from the building, and with the other he holds his weapon ready to keep the area secure.

Once on the ground, Blue Jay and Bean make a hasty departure.

"Get all three?" asks Bean as they move up the beach behind the hotel.

"Got the boss and one of his lieutenants. Missed the other one, but

I'm sure he will be in hot pursuit."

The two men continue up the beach a little longer, then cross over to the Nassau streets and proceed two blocks before turning left and up a dark narrow street. They will continue in this direction for a half mile, then turn left again and zigzag back to the Nassau waterfront.

Things at the Pink Palace are in a state of turmoil, and the people assigned to watch Jar Head and Doggie end their surveillance and return to the hotel. The surviving boss at the palace is in the process of organizing groups of men and sending them off to look for the assassins. After he gives a description of the man he saw briefly at the door, he sends them off in different directions. Cable Beach, Paradise Island and several groups head into the streets of Nassau, starting at the hotel and proceeding in different directions. After sending the groups out to hunt, the boss gives additional instructions to the men staying at the hotel before he and two other men leave to join the hunt.

In front of the hotel, a black Lincoln is parked at the curb. The three men approach it, get in, and the boss instructs the man behind the wheel to drive. As the Lincoln proceeds towards Cable Beach, the boss instructs everyone to be quiet so he can think. When the car comes to a stop at a traffic light, the boss is still trying to figure out where the assassins could have gone when he hears the faint sound of drums beating in the distance. "Make a U turn," he instructs the driver.

"Right now?" inquires the man behind the wheel.

"Right now."

The words are still in the air when the Lincoln jumps to life and makes the U-turn, cutting off a truck making a left turn at the corner as it completes its turn and proceeds back in the direction of the Pink Palace.

Blue Jay and Bean have been setting a fast pace, and are in the middle of an intersection when a black Lincoln turns the corner one block away and to their left. Blue Jay and Bean do not have a good feeling about this car, and with good reason. The boss has already decided to shoot down the two men in the car's headlights…and if it's a mistake, who cares.

As the car speeds up, Blue Jay and Bean break into a run and disappear around the corner. When the Lincoln gets to the intersection, it turns left to follow the two men. As it speeds down the street, a man in the back seat opens fire, almost hitting the two men on foot. Bean and Blue Jay decide it's time to start moving towards the waterfront, and run down a narrow alley. After jumping a few fences, they turn left and back in the direction they just came from.

When they get to the street, they turn right and proceed towards the waterfront.

The Lincoln drives to the next street before turning left to continue the chase. Not hearing or seeing anything, the boss figures the men doubled back, and the driver makes a left turn at the next street.

Blue Jay and Bean are two blocks from the waterfront when they start their zigzag routine as they proceed to their destination. The two men quickly turn right at the next corner and run right into a holiday parade that is proceeding down the main street. Between the people in the parade and the spectators on the sidewalk, they have to fight their way through the crowds. After proceeding four blocks, they are past the end of the parade. They turn left at the next street and right at the following one.

Between the parade and the zigzag route, Blue Jay and Bean should have been free from pursuit…but the new boss in the Lincoln had a feeling they would use the parade to cover their escape and the Lincoln is on the prowl, looking for the two men that eluded them earlier.

Bean and Blue Jay are in the middle of the block when the Lincoln appears at the intersection they just left. The new boss spots the two men walking, and the Lincoln makes a quick right turn in hot pursuit.

"These assholes again," remarks Bean as both men take cover behind a parked car.

"We have to do something about this," replies Blue Jay. As the Lincoln comes closer, Blue Jay and Bean send a hail of rounds at the windshield and side windows. The car stops and the four men inside get out and take cover behind it. Seconds later, return fire is coming back towards Blue Jay and Bean. After firing another volley the two men, using the parked cars for cover, continue up the street and disappear around the corner. Once out of sight, they split up. Bean ducks down an alley, and Blue Jay crosses to the other side of the street, continuing past a series of small storefronts.

The boss is not about to let these two get away again as he and his men give quick pursuit up the street. As they turn the corner, they catch sight of one of the men running down the other side of the street and start firing at him. With rounds hitting all around him, and with no cars to hide behind, Blue Jay ducks into a store front. Keeping very low, he fires one round. His thumb then presses the magazine release, and the magazine is allowed to drop a quarter of the way out of the handle of his weapon. That done, Blue Jay stands and fires another round at the four men on the other side of the street. Thinking the last shell casing was just ejected and the magazine is empty, the slide on his Blackhawk stays open to the rear and waits for a full magazine to be loaded.

The four men see this occur and quicken their pace, hoping to catch him during a reload.

Blue Jay kneels into a low position and waits.

When the four men approach the middle of the street, two men appear from around the far corner and immediately realize what is happening. One of their students has gotten himself cornered in a storefront doorway, and four men are moving in for the kill. Doggie and Jar Head draw their weapons, but before they can aim and fire they hear the muffled sounds of two rounds being fired from an alley halfway up the block, and one of the four men in the middle of the street goes down.

That's what Blue Jay was waiting for. His left palm slams the magazine back into the weapon, the right thumb presses the slide release, and as the slide clicks home he comes up firing. A second man drops, and Bean takes out a third. The only man standing is the new short-term boss. He now realizes he is in the middle of an ambush, and tries to figure his best course of action. It's a thought he will not complete-two rounds from opposite directions cut him down.

Doggie and Jar Head move up the block to make sure that Bean was the one doing the shooting from the alley as Blue Jay quickly checks the men in the middle of the street.

Bean appears from the alley and approaches the two teachers.

"Why were you two that far apart during the firefight?" inquires Jar Head. "Didn't we tell you during our training sessions to try and stay together?"

"Well, it seemed like a good idea at the time,"

Bean fires back.

"Well, it's back to class next week," Jar Head informs him as he and Doggie turn and proceed back the way they came.

Blue Jay has checked out the men in the street, and as he approaches Bean he inquires, "What did he say?"

"He said we're going back to Cool next week," Bean answers.

"Well I hope we get a chance to ride the Cool Bus this time."

With Jar Head and Doggie taking the lead and their students a quarter of a block behind, the four walk five blocks to their original rendezvous point. Once there, Blue Jay and Bean go into an alley, quickly change into different clothes and put the clothes they were wearing into a weighted sack.

When they reappear, each man is wearing light-colored clothing, a hat, and carrying a suitcase. The four men take a look around the area. Satisfied that nothing is out of order, Doggie motions for the students to continue down the waterfront.

First Blue Jay, then Bean starts the two-block walk, with the teachers taking up rear guard.

Once at the two-block mark, Blue Jay starts to cross the street. As they all know, the middle of the street is not a good place to be if someone is after you, and all are a little tense and jump as the ship's whistle sounds, alerting the passengers still in Nassau that the ship will be leaving in one hour. *I better check my shorts for a racing stripe when I get on board,* thinks Blue Jay as he continues toward the gangway. Once Blue Jay is close to the gangway, Bean takes the same course.

With the children safe onboard, Doggie and Jar Head each light up a cigar and walk over to the edge of the pier. While talking about how good the Cuban cigars are, they drop the weighted sack into the water. Having smoked their fine Cubans, the two men also head for the gangway.

Their vacation plans show them as flying to Nassau, spending a few days, picking up a cruise ship at Nassau that will tour the Caribbean, and returning to Florida. Bean and Blue Jay, on the other hand, are two of the people that missed the ship's departure in Florida and were joining the cruise at Nassau. After an hour and a whole lot of whistle blowing, the ship pulls away from its berth.

For the cruise, Doggie and Jar Head will travel together. Blue Jay and Bean will act out a chance meeting at the gangway and start talking about why they had missed the ship in Florida, or as Swabbie would say, *a shit-for-the-birds story,* and hang out together for the remainder of the cruise. The cruise is a good chance for all to unwind and enjoy the beauty of the Caribbean.

Once back in the U.S., Jar Head and Doggie catch a flight back to Washington, D.C., and their students do the same via Chicago.

Blue Jay and Bean are still staying at the Hilton up on Connecticut Avenue, and depend on Jar Head and Doggie for transportation to Langley each day.

As the two men stand on the street alongside the Hilton, a small blue bus pulls up and stops in front of them. The door opens, and Doggie steps off the bus and says, "You children get a move on. You don't want to be late for Cool."

Bean and Blue Jay look at each other and smile as they start to get onto the bus. Jar Head is behind the wheel, and informs the students as they climb the stairs of the bus, "The Agency doesn't have any yellow cool buses, so this one will have to do."

With the score for the morning joust at teachers 2, students 0,

Bean fires off a reply.

"A blue bus made by the Blue Bird Bus Company; what imagination, what creativity."

"I agree," adds Blue Jay. "It must be the result of one of those 'best suggestion' contests, with the winner being selected by a KGB double agent."

While the students continue on a roll, Jar Head looks at Bean and says, "Why don't I just drive up to teachers' leap and drive this bus over the cliff? It might save us a lot of future grief."

***

Two days later, the students have completed their field reports for the Nassau project and are sitting in Swabbie's office with their teachers discussing their first mission.

"How do you men feel about the way the project went?" Swabbie inquires to all.

Jar Head was the first to speak. "It was good up until the end," he starts. "They were too far apart, and put themselves into a dangerous crossfire situation. They were successful, but it was a poor choice of tactics."

"Any comments?" Swabbie asks.

"Yes," Blue Jay speaks up. "It may not be what our teachers would have done, but we were happy with the decision at the time and still are. We both know how to set up an ambush from opposite sides of the road, and to keep our fields of fire directed at the targets and not at each other."

"But this wasn't a situation out in the field; it was on a city street," counters Doggie.

"They're all dead, aren't they?" Bean fires back.

"Okay, okay," Swabbie intervenes. "It looks like we have a difference of opinion on this one, and I wasn't on-site so I can't make a judgement call. Let's move on."

"I have a question," Blue Jay says, raising a hand. "Why are we back in school?"

"Don't you feel the need?" asks Swabbie.

"No," Bean replies before Blue Jay can speak.

" How do you two feel about that?" Swabbie asks as he looks at Doggie and Jar Head.

"If they don't want to go back to COOL," Doggie suggests, "how about another exam?"

"Do you agree with that?" Swabbie asks Blue Jay and Bean.

Both men agree without even thinking about it.

"Since they feel like experts already," Jar Head announces, "we'll see how they do on a project with very little preparation for the mission."

Both students agree, and the meeting continues.

After Jar Head and Doggie confer at the conference table at the other end of the office, they return to their seats.

"Today is Thursday, September 23, 1993," Doggie says. "We will all leave together for Greece tomorrow. We know the identity of an enemy agent, code name Red Bird, who is working in the Athens area. We will put you in the area where Red Bird can be located. Your test will be to ID Red Bird ."

"Is that it?" asks Bean

"It's that or back to COOL," answers Jar Head

"That's plenty," Blue Jay assures the group, thinking to himself, *If we fail the test, at least we'll still get a few days' vacation in Athens before going back to COOL.*

The next night, all are seated on an international flight as it takes off from Dulles Airport just outside of Washington, D.C. It is an enjoyable flight, and all are looking out of the windows as the plane enters the final approach. Once their flight has landed the four men deplane, collect their luggage and are standing in line outside of the airport waiting for their turn at getting a cab.

About an hour later, the four men are checked into a hotel in downtown Athens and standing in the lobby discussing sightseeing they can take in.

"Jar Head and I have been here many times in the past, and there are a lot of things to see," Doggie volunteers.

"Yes, and I think you'll really enjoy the black-tie event we will be attending tonight." adds Jar Head.

"What black-tie event?" asks Blue Jay.

"Oh! Didn't we tell you?" Doggie inquires with fake concern. "Tonight at seven. See ya!" he says as the teachers walk away.

Bean and Blue Jay are a little pissed off, but head towards the desk to start tracking down two tuxedos.

Blue Jay and Bean are already outside looking up at the Acropolis when Doggie and Jar Head come out of the front doors of the hotel.

"It is impressive," Bean confirms.

"That's where we're going tonight," Jar Head informs him.

"Why in black tie?" asks Blue Jay

"We are going to a Yanni concert," answers Doggie. "Have you ever heard of him?"

"No," is the reply.

"You children don't get out much, do you?" Jar Head observes as he asks the doorman to hail a cab for them.

When the four men get to the concert, they file in and take their seats. First Bean; Blue Jay; Doggie; and finally Jar Head, bringing up the rear. A brief time after they are seated, the concert gets underway.

During the third presentation of the concert a violin solo is performed by a black women wearing a red dress and a matching red scarf to hold her hair in place on the top of her head. Halfway through the solo Bean, leans over toward the other three and asks, "Is Red Bird the women with the violin?"

"Yes," Doggie confirms.

"She isn't an agent, is she?" is the next question Bean asks.

"No," Jar Head answers, "this trip is a graduation present from your fathers."

Bean and Blue Jay are very surprised, and thank their Agency fathers for the gift as the third presentation comes to an end.

"I told you mine was smarter than yours," Doggie informs Jar Head.

"What did he say?" Bean asks Blue Jay, who is sitting closer to the other two.

"Your father said that I was smarter than you," Blue Jay replies.

"Yeah, like he would say something like that." Bean fires back. "You probably don't even know the difference between a violin and a viola."

"Yes I do," answers Blue Jay, "a viola burns longer."

When the students take a brief break during their discussion, Jar Head looks at the two, then at Doggie as he asks, "Do you think there's a retirement village nearby?"

The verbal combat in the audience is brought to a halt during the next presentation, when the bass player performs an excellent solo, followed by Red Bird who attempts to melt the strings on her violin. She performs exceptionally, and just when everyone thinks it is coming to an end, she takes it to new heights. Any higher, and only the local canines would be able to hear the notes.

As the concert continues, the two students start to understand why their mentors like this music. It is a new type and has an international flavor to it.

Yanni, the composer and star performer, has assembled other star performers, The Royal Philharmonic Orchestra and an excellent conductor to create a special night of music. It will without a doubt be remembered as one of the best concerts Yanni has ever created.

The trip and the concert are indeed great graduation gifts, and something that Blue Jay and Bean will remember for the rest of their lives.

CHAPTER SEVEN

T hree weeks have passed since the Nassau project, and the general has stopped making noises about replacing Jar Head and Doggie.

Since the DDO currently has four men in his special OPS unit, he decides to take on a project that is too much for a two-man unit, but four men could get the job done.

The DDO and the five men again meet in Swabbie's office around the conference table. Gil Dunn has just finished presenting the next project, and asks if there are any questions. With the exception of Blue Jay, everyone remains silent.

"What are the hard facts on why we should take this man out?" he inquires.

The DDO is not accustomed to this type of question at the first briefing, and especially from a new kid on the block.

"What do you mean?" asks Dunn.

"You've told us what a bad man this person is, but we have no hard intelligence to review."

"We usually do supply hard intel," answers Dunn, "but this one is so sensitive, the intel is on a need-to-know basis only. Have any problems with that?" the DDO asks, looking directly at Blue Jay.

"Well, yes I do," replies Blue Jay without hesitation, "With us not having access to all of the intel, we could be used to terminate people for political reasons."

The DDO's face starts to turn red as it changes from a nice expression to an NFL lineman's game face on Sunday afternoon.

"Are you saying I would let people be terminated for political reasons?" he erupts.

"Not necessarily you, but that type of procedure could be used by others in a bad way."

At this point Dunn is fuming, and the meeting moves from respectable to just short of a physical brawl, but Blue Jay will not back down. With the help of the other four men, things return to normal, and once again the DDO takes control of the meeting by announcing, "The intel on this one is on a need-to-know basis at a higher level, and that is the way it will stand." With that said, Dunn continues with the briefing. One hour later, the meeting is adjourned and everyone leaves Swabbie's office.

"Why do I have a bad feeling?" Jar Head asks Doggie.

"You mean about Blue Jay not getting access to the intel?" Doggie inquires. Jar Head shakes his head yes. "That thought passed through my head as well," Doggie relays to his partner.

Further down the hall, their Agency sons are heading for a cup of coffee. "You just have this thing about management, don't you?" asks Bean.

"I like to know the facts," answers Blue Jay. "*All* of the facts."

"Now, you know you're going to find out all the facts on your own anyway, so why ask?" replies Bean

"I like to give them the benefit of telling me when I ask," answers Blue Jay.

"I think you just want to piss them off," quips Bean

"That too."

***

After four weeks of preparation, a meeting is held in Swabbie's office to review the latest intelligence on the objective, and the plan to remove the same.

"Blue Jay, I know some weeks ago you had a problem with not having access to all of the intel on this project. Do you still have concerns?" Swabbie asks.

"No," replies Blue Jay, "I am satisfied it is a good project, and not just being done for political reasons."

"Good," replies Swabbie, pleased that Blue Jay has decided to take higher management at their word.

The review process is headed into its second hour when the door to Swabbie's office flies open, and an irate DDO enters the room.

"You just had to know, didn't you?" he yells as he looks Blue Jay right in the eye.

"About what?" asks Blue Jay innocently.

"What's the problem, Gil?" Swabbie inquires.

"Somehow, this rookie got into the files for this project that I had in my office," Dunn answers, still yelling.

"Why do you think it was me?" asks a puzzled Blue Jay.

"Because of this," the DDO answers as he throws a magazine onto the conference table. "I found it in my file."

Everyone at the meeting leans forward to get a better look at the magazine on the table, and are a little surprised when they see a baseball publication with the Toronto Blue Jay on the cover.

"Who do you think put this in my file?" the DDO inquires.

"A diehard baseball fan?" offers Blue Jay.

"You think it's funny, don't you?" Dunn again explodes.

"No."

"No!" Dunn echoes Blue Jay. "Well, I'll tell you one thing. I'm going to start a full-scale investigation, and I know that somewhere along the way you screwed up or got caught on videotape. When I find the proof, your ass is grass-and I'll be the lawnmower."

That said, Dunn leaves the office, slamming the door behind him.

"Well, that was fun," remarks Swabbie. "Blue Jay, did you get into his files?"

Before Blue Jay can answer, Jar Head speaks up.

"Swabbie, do you really want to know the answer to that question?"

Swabbie sits back in his chair for a second, then answers, "No. I'm too close to retirement. Forget I asked."

Doggie looks across the table at Jar Head and remarks, "I haven't seen a Deputy Director that pissed off since the time you had that little episode with the DDI."

"Like father, like son, I guess," adds Swabbie before Jar Head can respond to Doggie.

"Oh, so now *we're* the bad ones? See what you're doing to my reputation because of your run-in with the DDO?" Jar Head says to Blue Jay.

"Why is everyone so convinced it's me?" Blue Jay asks with an innocent look on his face.

"And another thing," adds Bean. "Why don't these people have any sense of adventure?"

"I think it's an age thing," replies Blue Jay

A moment of quiet settles over the group, then the silence is broken when Jar Head asks Doggie, "Did I tell you I decided to put a down payment on a little house I saw at the retirement village?"

"No, you didn't," replies Doggie, "but do me a favor and see if there are any empty houses in your neighborhood."

Swabbie is really enjoying this exchange. Jar Head and Doggie are usually busting on him, but now they have their hands full keeping up with their newfound sons.

***

One, and then two weeks pass with nothing said about the files or the magazine. The three older men are a little on edge. They all have worked with Dunn for many years, and know that if he finds anything, security will have Blue Jay in cuffs in no time.

Knowing they are a little on edge, Gert rushes into the room once in a while. This is done for their benefit, to help break the tension.

Seeing them all jump is for her benefit. Everyone knows both reasons, and all get a good laugh each time she does it.

It is the middle of the third week when the DDO asks for a briefing on the project. When all are gathered in his office, Dunn inquires, "This is your first visit to my office since you came on board, isn't it, Bean?"

"Yes, it is," confirms Bean.

Then Dunn just looks at Blue Jay as he walks past him on the way to the conference table in his office.

Once everyone is seated, Dunn asks Swabbie to start the briefing. Everything moves along smoothly with questions, answers and concerns about the project.

They know that one of two things has happened concerning the file and magazine episode. Either Dunn can't find anything that points to Blue Jay, or he has found something but is so impressed with how Blue Jay did it, he doesn't want to pursue the matter and lose a good operative.

After Swabbie completes the briefing he asks the DDO if he has any questions.

"No," answers Dunn, "it's a good plan, but I would feel better if you drew up some additional contingency plans."

"I'll look into it," Swabbie answers quickly.

"When will you start the project?" is the DDO's next question.

"With your approval, next week." answers Swabbie.

"Then next week it is, and good luck to you all," confirms Dunn.

"I have another request for Jar Head and Doggie," Dunn continues. "Make sure you bring these kids back with you. They make this place a little more lively when they're around."

"We'll do our best," the two old salts assure the DDO as all stand and leave his office.

CHAPTER EIGHT

I t is a dark night as a black rubber raft approaches the island of Sardinia off the coast of Italy. Since they are using two electric motors, the only thing that can be heard are small waves slapping against the front of the raft as it moves through the Mediterranean Sea. With Jar Head in the front of the raft and Doggie manning the motor, the raft slows to a crawl when it is approximately 50 yards from the beach.

The U.S.S. Shark Fin is standing by in case a hasty retreat has to be made after the four men in the raft get to the beach. After surfacing and getting the raft underway, the sub again submerges to a point where only its tower is halfway out of the water. If they are picked up on radar by another ship, they will probably be mistaken for a small boat. When the sub submerges fully, radar operators will probably believe it to be a ghost echo...and at 4 a.m., unless there's a war on or someone is calling for help, who cares.

At 25 yards, Doggie cuts the motors and lets the raft drift as the four men survey the beach. As covered in the planning stage, each man is wearing night-vision gear and is slowly checking the portion of the beach he was assigned. Once everyone is satisfied the beach is clear, Doggie starts the electric motors and slowly moves towards the beach. Five minutes later, the motors have been disconnected and put into the craft, and the four men are quickly removing the raft from the beach.

That completed, Bean and Blue Jay return to the beach and sweep the sand clear of four sets of footprints. While Jar Head is breaking out the camouflage netting that will be used to conceal the raft, Doggie is on the radio to the sub. No voice communication is required. He presses the send button four times: two long, then two short. The sub pulls the plug and disappears into the Mediterranean Sea without changing its position. Once fully submerged, the Shark Fin gets underway and to its assigned patrol.

When Blue Jay and Bean return from the beach, the four men pick up the raft and move further off the beach. Once satisfied they are far enough away, they start looking for a place to conceal it. A little further on, they find a group of bushes and place the raft beside them. After removing all of their gear from the raft, Doggie and Jar Head spread the camouflage netting over the raft and are securing it while Bean and Blue Jay leave to gather foliage and do some selective pruning of the bushes in the area.

When they return, the netting is in place and Doggie is removing a map from his backpack. "We'll finish with the raft," Bean informs the other two as he and Blue Jay drop their loads of foliage that will be used to conceal the raft. The two older men acknowledge the statement, take the map and move about twenty yards further inland to the edge of a clearing. Daylight is replacing the pitch black of night as the men unfold the map and lay it on the ground.

"I see it's still hills and rocks," observes Jar Head.

"Hasn't changed much, has it?" Doggie replies.

After working with the map and a compass for awhile, Doggie and Jar Head are satisfied they're in the right place. There are easier ways to do this, but these two are old-fashioned...and besides, technology takes the fun out of everything.

When they rejoin the other two, the task of concealing the raft is completed and it has become part of the group of bushes.

"Nice job," remarks Jar Head.

"Yes, it is," agrees Doggie. "I hope we can find it on our return trip."

"No problem," Bean answers quickly as he removes a global positioning finder from his pack.

After hitting a few buttons he has their location.

"Technology," Doggie says as he shakes his head.

"No fun doing it that way," offers Jar Head.

"I have to agree with them," Blue Jay speaks up. "There is nothing more enjoyable, while being pursued on a dark night in the rain, than stopping to get out your map and compass to find out where in the fuck you are."

Bean starts to laugh as he puts the finder back into his pack.

"Smart-ass kids with their tech toys," Jar Head announces.

"They probably don't even know how to use a compass," adds Doggie.

"Pa and Pa Kettle don't like our toy," Bean tells his partner.

"I know," Blue Jay agrees, then asks, "How come you Kettle brothers haven't moved into the twentieth century yet?"

"I'll give you Kettle brothers," Jar Head announces as he and Doggie pick up their packs, each wearing a big smile on their face.

"Okay! The map and compass say we should go in this direction. Is that all right with you technologists?"

Doggie inquires.

"Lead on," answers Bean.

"You always have to piss off management, don't you?" inquires Blue Jay.

"Oh, that's really funny, coming from you," answers Bean.

Being in a remote and isolated part of the island, this type of humorous bickering can go on, but once the four start moving, it will be different.

"Ready?" Jar Head asks. Everyone acknowledges with a yes.

"Let's move out," Jar Head says as he takes the lead.

The team has decided to use a four-man diamond formation and rotate positions from time to time. The front of the diamond will lead the team towards the objective, and will probably be the first to discover anything out of the ordinary. The left and right side will cover the flanks, and the back of the diamond will act as a rear guard. In this formation, three of the four men can bring fire in any direction without hesitation while the fourth man moves to help or holds his position as a security measure.

'Rocks and hills' is an understatement. One of the reasons the landing spot is so isolated is that there are no roads or even a path in the area. It is truly surrounded by hills and rocks…big rocks. Each winter and spring, the rains come down so heavy that it seems the island will melt into the Mediterranean.

The team will move during daylight hours on this part of the island, but when they start getting closer to the objective they will switch to night travel.

There are fourteen miles from the point they came ashore to the objective. After they travel the first dozen or so miles, the team holds up in a small cave until nightfall. No need to review plans; everyone knows what is expected of him, so they pass the time by double-checking weapons and surveying the valley below.

With the arrival of nightfall, the four men put on their kill suits and night vision gear, and leave the small cave. It is a bit early to start the patrol, but the team has to make sure the target is in residence before any action is taken. If the target is not there, or it cannot be determined whether he's there, the team will withdraw and move on to another location to wait until the next night. The first night, the target cannot be located, and the team withdraws and proceeds to the other side of the residence. At daybreak, the four men are concealed in an area of heavy foliage and keeping the residence under surveillance, looking for signs of the target.

"I don't get it." Blue Jay says.

"Don't get what?" asks Jar Head.

"Why Dunn thinks we need four men for this job. It doesn't seem like it's going to be that hard."

"We already covered his security force in our briefings and how we will have to get in close to get at this guy, but let me put it a different way." Jar Head explains. "When we start the activities, men will come out of that residence like roaches running from a can of Raid. You may think they're disorganized, but you would be wrong. Each man will be running to his defensive position in order to repel any attack. Each is armed with a semi-automatic weapon with a selector switch for full automatic fire, and they know how to use their weapons. The trick is to hit the target, hit the security force hard, and keep them off balance long enough to escape."

"You've been here before, haven't you?" asks Blue Jay.

"Ten years ago," Jar Head replies. "We hit him, but it wasn't a fatal wound and we almost bought the farm instead."

"We were shittin' and gettin' that night," adds Doggie, "and got away by the skins of our asses."

"Let me guess," Bean interjects. "The last time you were here, you two got on line, charged the residence yelling and shooting, then got a surprise when the cockroaches came running out."

"Yeah, sort of like what we have planned for this time, only we know about the cockroaches," Doggie says.

Blue Jay gets Bean's attention, then says, "Did I tell you I checked out a house in one of those swinging singles villages?"

"Now why are you thinking about that? We're probably going to get killed tonight, or tomorrow at the latest," Bean replies.

"You're right; what was I thinking about?" agrees Blue Jay.

Doggie and Jar Head continue scanning the area through powerful scopes for signs of the target, but are also enjoying the conversation.

That afternoon, Doggie thinks he has spotted the objective and informs the others: "At 9 o'clock; the table with the umbrella." Jar Head quickly grabs a scope and finds the man in question.

"That's him," he confirms. "Let's break out the stuff."

***

It is 8:15 p.m., and the four are in position. Blue Jay and Bean will take out the target while Jar Head and Doggie keep the cockroaches off balance. Blue Jay and Bean move around the area, looking and waiting for the target to appear. If they see him at a window, they will stagger their shots. First Bean will fire, to break the window or weaken bullet-resistant glass. A split second later Blue Jay will fire.

After another hour, the four men are starting to wonder how long they will be able to avoid detection by the security patrols. Another

30 minutes pass before the target finally appears in front of a picture window, stopping to light up a cigar.

Unfortunately, at that same moment a two-man security patrol has just come into view about 25 yards from the two men in the bushes.

Bean and Blue Jay slowly remove their 9mm Berettas from their holsters and stick them under their belts in the front of their pants. This done, both men take aim at the target and Bean, then Blue Jay fires. Both rounds penetrate the glass, find their target, and the man is terminated.

After firing, Bean draws his 9mm pistol, falls forward on the ground and starts shooting at the two security men on patrol. Ascertaining the target has been dispatched, Blue Jay draws his pistol, turns to the left and also engages the security patrol. Being caught completely by surprise, the security men are slow to react and go down after a few volleys. Doggie and Jar Head start by firing their M-79 grenade launchers at every doorway they can see. Some of the grenades reach the doors and explode just as the cockroaches are trying to come out. On the other side of the residence, the other half of the team tosses four frag grenades at the residence and move off.

After firing a few more rounds of M-79s,, Jar Head and Doggie start to move off as well.

When the explosions have stopped for a few seconds, the cockroaches are in quick pursuit and charging the area where the grenades were being launched. A few seconds later, five more of the security force are taken out by a Claymore mine that has been set off by a trip wire. These security people are not quitters, and they keep coming. Doggie and Jar Head don't waste any time in their retreat, but are surprised by a four-man group from the security force that had taken another route and were about to cut off their escape.

The security people can't see their prey, but they can hear them and start firing in the direction of the noise. Doggie and Jar Head hit the deck as rounds start landing all around them. The men keep firing and moving towards the place they heard the noise; then two shots from heavy-caliber weapons ring out, and two of the security people fall to the ground. As the two remaining men turn to meet their new enemy, they are also taken out.

"Must be our sons," Jar Head exclaims as both men get to their feet and continue on their escape route. A short time later, they are joined by Blue Jay and Bean.

"They still coming?" Jar Head inquires.

"No, they finally gave up, but I wouldn't stick around this area too long," Blue Jay offers, and with that said the four men continue to the raft.

The sky in the east is light, dawn is just minutes away, and the four men are still two miles from the location of the raft. They had to wait longer than expected to get the shot, and are running behind schedule. The four men are within one mile of the raft when they hear what sounds like a helicopter approaching from behind them. If they were in a foliage area they could just get down and wouldn't be seen. Unfortunately they are on the upside of a hill, with very little of anything growing on it.

"Get to the downside," yells Doggie, and the four men climb the remainder of the hill as fast as they can on legs that already feel like rubber bands.

Just as they get to the top, the helicopter gets them into view and heads straight for them as the man in the seat next to the pilot starts talking on the radio. As the 'copter approaches them it swings to the right, then back to the left, and automatic weapons fire at them from the side door. The four on the ground jump over the crest of the hill to the downside as the 'copter maneuvers for another pass.

The men are half way down the hill when the bird passes again. At the bottom of the hill Jar Head motions for everyone to stop and says, "We have to give that bird something to think about while we make our move across this open area and to the foliage on the other side."

All agree, and get ready for the next pass. As the copter approaches, Bean and Blue Jay take aim at the pilot and the men in the doorway while Jar Head and Doggie prepare to spray the bird with automatic weapons fire. When the bird gets into range, the four open up. One man in the doorway drops and a hole appears in the window in front of the pilot. That, with the hits from automatic weapons, makes the pilot pull the bird into a sharp right turn and out of harm's way. When he does this, the four men on the ground hall ass across the open area and into the foliage, out of sight of the helicopter.

With less than a mile to go, the team moves on and in a short time are approaching the raft area. Things seem to be working out until Bean looks out to sea and discovers two speedboats heading towards the beach. "That's who the guy in the copter was talking to, and they've probably landed behind us."

"Let's get to the raft and lay low," Jar Head announces, "If they pass us we can steal their boats and make for the extraction point."

All agree, and a few minutes later are in place around the raft. The two boats have landed on the beach, and one of the men is talking on the radio. When he stops talking, the crews spread out and proceed off the beach in search of the four men.

As they move inland, five of the ten men are heading straight for the raft, and there is no chance they'll miss it.

The four men around the raft are just about to start one hell of a firefight when the undergrowth comes to life with 9mm automatic weapons fire, and six of the ten men drop immediately. Before the other four can react, they are also dispatched. Then everything grows quiet. A few second later, a large piece of undergrowth stands up and approaches the four that were on the run.

"Seal Team," he reports. "Someone by the name of Gil asks us to sit on your point of departure in case there was any trouble. Your mode of transportation has also been changed to one of our boats. It will be here very soon." Jar Head and Doggie are very impressed with what just happened, and shake hands and thank the young officer. Bean and Blue Jay also shake hands and thank him. They have seen this type of well-executed action before, and maybe someday they will be able to return the favor.

Thirty minutes later, the four men and the Seal Team are on two high-speed boats, hauling ass across the Mediterranean away from Sardinia. They will hook up with one of the ships of the sixth fleet they are assigned to, and once the speedboats are hoisted onboard they will get underway. Two days at sea, a brief stop at a U.S. Naval facility in the Mediterranean, and the foursome are on a military flight that is making its final landing approach at Andrews Air Force Base just outside of Washington, D.C.

"I guess we'll be dining at Harvey's tonight," Doggie says to Jar Head.

"That's a given," he replies.

"I think it's time for our Agency Sons to meet the Ladies, don't you?"

"Good idea," approves Jar Head. "Maybe with their younger eyes they can keep the Ladies from 'borrowing' Harvey's utensils for home use?" Doggie gives out a big laugh, and the two start telling the tale of the three Ladies and the lobster picks.

When Jar Head and Doggie come back from a project, dinner the first night is usually at Harvey's with Swabbie and the Ladies. They always have a good time, with lots of laughs. With the addition of Bean and Blue Jay to the group, things will be rocking and rolling at Harvey's tonight.

CHAPTER NINE

The next day at Langley finds the father-and-son teams a little more quiet than usual. Between the project and last night at Harvey's, they are regrouping. After working on their field reports for a few hours, Jar Head announces, "Let's go to Swabbie's office. We think it's time to tell you two about some other concerns we all have."

Swabbie is sitting at his desk when Gert buzzes the intercom. "Yes, Gert?" he says.

"The Dynamic Foursome are here to see you," Gert informs him.

"Send them in," Swabbie replies.

As the two senior men move towards the office door, Doggie announces, "It used to be the Dynamic Duo."

"Yeah, I know," Jar Head confirms, "I think it should be the Dynamic Duo and Trainees."

"Or Dynamic Duo and Interns," offers Doggie.

Bean and Blue Jay are still standing at Gert's desk as the other two enter Swabbie's office.

"Sorry about that," Gert offers.

"That's okay, Gert," Blue Jay assures her. "I'll just have to do or say something today to piss them both off." He also heads for the office door.

"See what I have to put up with, Gert?" Bean complains. "Two old farts and a smartass."

Gert, who was still giggling at Blue Jay's remark, bursts out laughing.

"Hey! Leave our woman alone," a voice sings out.

Bean looks towards Swabbie's office and finds Jar Head and Doggie standing just inside the door way. "Dam kids, you have to watch them every minute," complains Doggie.

"Well, you spoil them," Jar Head announces as both men turn and move back to Swabbie's desk.

"I have to go now," Bean informs Gert, and she makes a waving gesture to pass him through and into the office so she can stop laughing and catch her breath.

When the men are all seated around Swabbie's conference table, Jar Head is the first to speak, "By the way, before we start the briefing, we want to thank you for the Seal Team at the beach."

"That was the DDO's idea," answers Swabbie. "I think his exact words were, 'I don't want anything to happen to that smart-ass kid before we have a chance to go another round or two.'"

"The Seal Team leader did say somebody by the name of Gil asked them to sit on the departure point," offers Doggie.

"I guess that means we are going to see more clashes between those two," Jar Head says.

"What are your thoughts about that?" Swabbie asks Jar Head.

"I'm going out to pasture."

"How about you, Blue Jay?" Swabbie inquires.

"My thoughts are," Blue Jay replies, "If he can't take a joke, fuck him."

"Good," Swabbie smiles. "I was just taking a status check to make sure nothing had changed. Do you think Anne will like the Village?" Swabbie asks Jar Head.

"Give her two weeks with these two and she'll love it," Jar Head assures Swabbie.

A few more minutes of jousting and the meeting turns from humor to deadly serious as the others start to brief Bean and Blue Jay.

***

"I'll give you an overview on the topic, then we can get into detail," Swabbie starts. "We have a strong feeling that someone, either in or connected with the Agency, is playing for the other side." Swabbie continues, "Some of our projects, as well as projects from other departments, have been compromised-and people have died as a result. The DDO is trying to ferret out any person or persons that may be responsible, but to date has been unsuccessful. If they exist, they are very good at concealing their operation."

"You say *if* they exist," interjects Bean. "What makes you think they do exist?"

"We have good reasons to think this is the case,"

Swabbie tells him. "For one thing, Doggie and Jar Head came close to getting terminated on a project shortly before you two came on board. The opposition was waiting in ambush just off the beach in the middle of the night, and these two had a hard time getting away."

This piece of information really gets Blue Jay and Bean's attention, and both sit up straighter and start asking questions about who could be doing it and how. A lot of joking goes on between the teachers and the students, but under the surface the four have developed a deep friendship. Blue Jay and Bean are full-time interested in anyone that has tried, or will try, to terminate their mentors.

The briefing is going into its second hour when Gert buzzes the office, alerting the group that they are about to have company. Twenty seconds later, the door to the office swings open and the DDO walks in.

"I see you made it back in one piece," he observes.

"Yes, sir," answers Jar Head. "It was getting a little tight at the end, but that Seal Team took out all the remaining opposition."

"Good!" replies Dunn, knowing that statement is a thank-you for having the Seal Team at the departure point.

"We were bringing Bean and Blue Jay up to speed on the possibility of a double agent in or around the Agency."

"I have been checking out everything that looks a little out of the ordinary, and have come up with nothing," Dunn says as he joins the conversation. The six men are having a good discussion, and even Dunn and Blue Jay seem to be getting along better.

Another hour passes before Dunn's beeper goes off and he is forced to leave to attend to other matters. As he prepares to leave, Blue Jay speaks up.

"Mr. Dunn, Bean and myself want to thank you for your help with the Sardinia project."

"Time out," says Dunn, forming the letter T with his two hands. "Mr. Dunn," he repeats. "Are you trying to be nice to me?"

"Well...yes," answers Blue Jay.

"Well stop it, you're scaring me," Dunn tells him, then asks, "Does this mean you will not be referring to me as 'Fuck Face Dunn' any more?"

Blue Jay and Bean act surprised when Dunn asks the question. "Don't give me that surprised look," Dunn says. "I didn't get to be DDO because I'm a dumb-ass that keeps his head in the sand." Dunn then looks at the other three men at the table and announces, "I liked these kids better when they were bad."

"Well, sir, if that's the case, we'll try to get your admiration back," Blue Jay assures the DDO.

As Dunn approaches the door he turns back to the group and announces, "Swabbie, I owe Doggie and Jar Head for bringing the kids back safe and sound. Why don't you three join me around four o'clock, and we'll go hoist a few. Bring the children too; I guess they are old enough to drink soda pop." Dunn then turns and continues to leave the office. As he passes Gert's desk he is chuckling to himself. Gert sees this and immediately clicks on the intercom to see what is going on.

Since he and Dunn seemed to be getting along better, Blue Jay is caught totally off guard by his remarks, and the DDO is out of the office before he could fully recover. Dunn had planned it that way and can hardly wait for the future rebuttal. Blue Jay is starting to regroup as the other four men look at him, waiting for his next words.

"Children; we're children again," Blue Jay informs Bean. "Children and soda pop. Well, pop this, Gilbert," Blue Jay announces, and the room erupts into laughter.

When the room gets quiet again Bean says, "I don't understand why you're getting so upset. Your Uncle Gillie said he would buy the soda pop."

"Whose side are you on, anyway?" Blue Jay asks.

"I don't know; I get confused."

"It's contagious," observes Doggie. "Now my son is starting to act up. Can we call in sick for this drinks after work thing?" he continues.

"How about if you tell Dunn we had to go check out some new intel on the Japanese planning an attack on Hong Kong?" adds Jar Head.

"It will be okay," Swabbie assures them, knowing it is going to be an interesting evening. He figures Blue Jay is already planning his attack, and Dunn a counter-attack. Swabbie just hopes it doesn't get too interesting and the DDO decides to shit-can them all.

***

The next morning, having survived the drinks after work engagement, Swabbie and the Dynamic Foursome are again meeting in his office.

"Well how do you feel about your Uncle Gilbert this morning?" Bean asks his partner.

"He's okay," answers Blue Jay. "I think he just likes to piss me off."

"I have been watching that situation a little closer and have an analogy," Jar Head announces. "A man reaches down and pinches a young lad's nose, and laughs. The young lad kicks the man in the shins, the man starts yelling, and then the lad starts laughing. Then they start all over again. Am I close?" he inquires.

"You're right on the money," confirms Doggie, and everyone in the room agrees.

***

Weeks pass with no headway made on identifying the double agent, and planning is underway for the next project. This time, Bean and Blue Jay will be on their own--but not until a very long planning process where Blue Jay and Bean are at the helm, with Doggie and

Jar Head taking up review and advisory roles.

It is a quiet day at Langley. Dunn is in England, meeting with his counterpart in British Intelligence. Swabbie and Anne are on a cruise ship in the Caribbean enjoying an overdue vacation.

Bean and Blue Jay are at another Agency facility researching their next project, while Doggie and Jar Head man the fort and have taken up residence in Swabbie's office.

At 12:30 p.m., the gray phone rings in Swabbie's office and Doggie answers it.

"Yes, General," Doggie says, alerting Jar Head, who is on another phone. After listening for a time, Doggie replies, "But General, that plan is still in its early stages, and this will be their first time out."

After listening a while longer, Doggie offers, "Maybe we should contact the DDO."

Jar Head can hear the general's voice from across the room as he replies to that suggestion. A few seconds later, Doggie hangs up the phone.

"What's up?" asks Jar Head.

"They want to move the project up to right now," Doggie answers.

"I smell something," Jar Head says. "The timing alone makes it stink. Dunn in London, Swabbie on a cruise ship. I think somebody planned it that way."

"I know," agrees Doggie, "but is it the general making a play to try and get his team into the project, or is it a setup?"

"I think it's the latter," offers Jar Head.

"I agree," says Doggie.

"Well, we had to learn under fire and on our own. We didn't have much training, either," states Jar Head. "Hey, life's rough."

"So you're saying we're going in their place?" Doggie inquires.

"That's the way I see it," Jar Head confirms. "We can't send them into a possible ambush. Besides, we've been ambushed before and survived."

Doggie gets on the intercom and asks Gert to come into the office. After explaining to her what was going on, they ask her to run interference for them, but explain it could mean trouble for her, and how they would understand if she didn't what to do it. Gert's reply is just a look…probably the same look she gave that mugger before she chased him down the street. Jar Head and Doggie look at Gert, then at each other, smile and continue.

One of the things Gert will do is give the general the runaround when he starts looking for them, or for Blue Jay and Bean. With the secretary in agreement with her part of the plan, Gert and the Dynamic Duo stand and leave the office.

At Gert's desk the three stop to say goodbye, and Gert wishes them good luck. Jar Head and Doggie can see Gert is concerned about their safety, and try to lighten the mood. Standing next to Gert on either side, they give her a hug and Doggie says, "Gert, if the general comes down here and starts giving you a hard time, just put on that face you showed us when we asked, 'if you don't want to do this, we will understand'."

"Yeah! That will scare the shit out of him," Jar Head adds.

The three laugh, and the Duo are on their way--but Gert still doesn't have a good feeling about this one.

CHAPTER TEN

Doggie and Jar Head have been through this drill so many times, they could probably do it in their sleep. A plan in development with an execution date a few months away, then suddenly it's an early go. For this project, they allowed a long lead time to let Blue Jay and Bean get up to speed for their first solo project. Doggie and Jar Head filling in for the other two is something the person setting them up didn't plan on.

Having performed these projects for so many years, Doggie and Jar Head have developed a good relationship with the Special OPS Support Group, and they do not question things when these two change or add things to the mission support side of things.

When they showed up and told the support group they were filling in for Blue Jay and Bean, no questions were asked. Even when the two insisted on signing a document stating they were taking full responsibility for the replacements, they were told that wouldn't be necessary. The group knew and respected these two, and would bend or even break the rules for them.

"We have a unique situation," Doggie informs the group. "This project may be on the up-and-up, but we have a bad feeling about it, and feel it isn't fair to send Blue Jay and Bean out on what may be a set-up." The group shakes their heads in agreement. They, too, have noticed strange happenings on some of the missions, and were starting to question the reasons.

"We are taking off now, but once people become aware we are filling in they will probably try to recall us, so we'll require some communications problems," Jar Head requests.

"Who are the people that may be calling?" asks the head of the group.

"At first, shitheads and bad people. After a while, good people," answers Jar Head.

The group knows that the 'good people' are probably Swabbie and the DDO, and 'after a while' means they are probably out of position, and someone is taking advantage of that fact.

"No problem," answers the Support Section Chief. "It's not the first time we've had communications problems. Let me rig you both up with secondary communications gear, in case you have to talk with us."

As Doggie and Jar Head go with him to collect their com gear, Jar Head looks at the Section Chief's hair and points out, "Getting a little gray, aren't we?"

"Yes," answers the Chief, "and most of it is thanks to you two."

"Chief! Bubbie! How can you say that?" asks Doggie.

"How can I say that?" echoes the Chief. "Over the years, I have probably lied to almost all of the Agency's management for you two. Come to think of it, I better retire before they catch up with me."

"Did I tell you I am looking into a retirement village myself?" asks Jar Head. "Oh yes, I am; and Doggie wants me to check my street for any empty houses so he can take up residence."

"Well, find one for me while you are at it. I'm getting too old for this shit, and those two you're getting up to speed look like they're going to be worse than you two."

"We can only hope," Doggie says.

The three men laugh as they enter the hallway that leads to the communications section.

After going over the game plan and getting their special com gear, Jar Head, Doggie and the Chief visit other units to collect what they will need for this project. Backpacks, automatic weapons, sidearms, and a few other goodies; and they are ready to leave when Jar Head exclaims, "We forgot the tools!"

"That's right," agrees Doggie, and both men turn to retrieve them.

"What tools?" a newer member of the section asks the Chief.

"Entrenching tools," answers the Chief, "but don't ask me why. They have been taking them on every project since I've been here. Maybe they dig for treasure while they're waiting for pickup,"

As the Chief finishes talking, the two reappear with their tools attached to their backpacks.

"Are you happy now?" the Chief inquires.

"Very," Doggie replies.

"I'm driving you to the strip," the Chief informs the two. "I want to keep these youngsters out of this one as much as possible. If you two screw up, I don't want to get them into trouble."

"Well thanks for the vote of confidence Chief," Doggie grumbles.

***

"Yeah! If you two screw up!" adds Jar Head

The three men again laugh, and head for the 4x4 and the ride to the airstrip. The men in the section watch as the Chief, Doggie and Jar Head get into the 4x4 and drive out of the building. They know if any heat comes down from the top, the Chief will try to protect them. They also know if it comes to that, they are all in it together, no matter what the Chief tells them.

It doesn't take long to get to a small, remote airstrip, and the Chief brings the 4x4 to a stop close to a waiting helicopter. After a brief discussion the two pilots board the craft and fire up the engine.

"Thanks for everything, Chief," Jar Head calls.

"Are you sure you don't want something in writing from us?" asks Doggie.

"Don't worry about it," the Chief replies, "just get your old asses back here in one piece. We have to check out some houses at the Village."

Doggie and Jar Head both laugh and shake hands with the Chief before boarding the craft. The helicopter transports them to Andrews Air Force Base and a waiting business jet. Then, it's off to Central America.

It is early morning when the business jet is on final approach at a remote airstrip in Honduras. This airstrip was used a lot when the Sandinista government was in power and Cuban troops were stationed in Nicaragua. It is still maintained, but traffic is a fraction of what it was in years past.

On request from the two operatives arriving on the jet, a helicopter is on the pad and ready to go. After a short briefing, Doggie and Jar Head will continue their journey.

The jet comes to a halt in front of several buildings along the strip, and before the turbos can come to a complete stop, Jar Head and Doggie are off the plane and heading for the largest building.

As they approach the front door, a young man with military bearing comes out to meet them.

"Morning," the man greets the two new arrivals. "I have everything laid out and ready to review."

"Hello, Jack. I'm glad to see you are still here," Doggie says. "This one could get a little interesting."

After the three men enter the building, they proceed to the second floor and a room used for briefings prior to a mission. The helicopter pilots and crew are already reviewing a map spread out on a large conference table. As Jar Head and Doggie enter the room, four familiar faces look up from the map to greet them.

"Someone in the States mentioned something about this project, and we thought familiar faces would ease your minds a little and let you concentrate on the mission itself," Jack announces.

"We appreciate it," says Jar Head as he and Doggie move to shake hands with the crew.

Doggie and Jar Head are happy to see the four men. They had worked with them several times in the past, and know they are all good people.

With the greetings out of the way, all gather around the map.

"We know the location, but can't figure out why it was moved up. It doesn't seem to be an urgent matter," Jack informs the two new arrivals.

"'Why' is a very good question," Doggie replies.

Knowing they can trust these men, Doggie and Jar Head inform them of Dunn and Swabbie being out of town, how this project was moved up for no apparent reason, and that they have a bad feeling about it. Jar Head concludes with, "It wasn't that long ago that you people had to come out and pluck us out of the sea as we paddled away from an ambush at another location."

The crew all shake their heads as they give additional thoughts to what was being said.

"We'll hang in the area as long as fuel allows after you get on the island," the senior pilot announces. "After that, just give us a call."

"We appreciate it," Jar Head and Doggie acknowledge the statement.

After a little more discussion, the pilots and crew go to the helicopter while Doggie and Jar Head accompany Jack.

As they all enter the armory, Jack announces, "I have you down for ammo, C-4 and detonators."

"That's about it," Jar Head confirms.

"How about if we take a few of these?" Doggie asks as he looks into an open box of hand grenades.

"Help yourself," Jack approves as he helps Jar Head put C-4 into his backpack.

Once Jar Head's pack is loaded he moves to the grenades and also puts four in his backpack, then closes the flap and buckles it shut as Doggie does the same with his pack.

After drawing ammunition for their sidearms and automatic weapons, they are ready to go and Jack leads the way to the helicopter pad. The pilots and crew are standing a short distance from the craft, enjoying a smoke before the flight. As the three men approach them they put out their smokes and move to the helicopter. Once there, the seven men huddle for any last minute questions or concerns, then all climb aboard. Jar Head and Doggie turn and say goodbye to Jack and climb aboard the craft. He wanted to go along, but figured his additional weight would use up fuel that would be better used hovering in the drop-off area. With everyone aboard, the helicopter engines are fired up; shortly after that rotors start to turn and Jack backs away from the craft.

Within 45 seconds the helicopter lifts off the ground and Jack extends his hand over his head in a farewell gesture. The nose of the craft dips down a little as it picks up forward speed along the landing strip, then banks to the right and out to sea towards its destination.

CHAPTER ELEVEN

The project is an arms-for-drugs operation on the island of Cayos, off the coast of Nicaragua. The objective is to take out the main man and do as much damage as possible to the facilities. Arms-for-drugs is not unusual for this part of the world, and isn't high on the Agency's priority list, but when the arms are going to Cuban-sponsored rebels it moves higher up the list. The original inhabitants on the island, the Miskitos, make up a large part of the population, and a contingent of the very wealthy have also taken up residence, explaining why some of the keys on the island are privately owned.

The objective has an estate along the coast on the eastern side of the island, and a warehouse a half-mile inland. The plan is to place the C-4 with time-delayed detonators at the warehouse, then move to the estate and try to locate the main man. If unsuccessful, they will position themselves and wait for the warehouse to blow. During the initial confusion, he may show himself. If not, Jar Head and Doggie will execute plan 'B' and go into the main house after him.

The helicopter is approaching from the north, and will land its passengers four miles down the coast from their objective. The helicopter is equipped with pontoons, so it can land on water. They have come in handy more than once when returning to base from an extended distance during an insertion or extraction of agents. When they are three miles out, the helicopter drops down low and is almost touching the water as it speeds to its destination. One mile out, the craft slows down to avoid additional rotor noise caused by a quick stop.

The beach is wide at the insertion point and allows the craft to land. When the pontoons touch the beach, Jar Head and Doggie are out and quickly get out of the open. The helicopter immediately lifts off and again the nose dips down as the craft races down the beach. They are in communication with the agents, and will stay in the immediately area until they know it is not an ambush. Then they will move over the horizon and hover as long as fuel allows in case they are needed.

Jar Head and Doggie check out the immediate area as the

helicopter slowly patrols back and forth along the beach. The two-man crew also serves as door gunners, one on each side, and is manning M-60 machine guns mounted in the doorway.

When the two agents are satisfied it is not a setup, they notify the pilots and crew, *it's okay,* and the craft proceeds to its position over the horizon.

Doggie and Jar Head have found good cover, and wait until the helicopter has been gone for at least five minutes. When they see no signs of movement, they slowly crawl to their right and out of the area. If it is a setup, it will be better to engage the enemy on one of their flanks instead of going into the middle to be surrounded and cut off from the beach.

When they are sure no ambush is in place, the two men stand and move slowly for a short distance, then pick up speed. A mile up the coast they stop to put on their kill suits and add additional undergrowth native to the island to camouflage their movements, and then continue their trek. After traveling another two miles, the beach starts a long curve to the right, and they can see the estate through their binoculars.

After surveying the area around the estate, they change direction, from north to north-by-northwest and the location of their first objective: the warehouse.

It is late afternoon when they approach the area of the warehouse. Doggie and Jar Head are moving low and slow as they look for a good vantage point to observe and wait for darkness to arrive. As they move in, a muffled sneeze is heard coming from their left front.

The two men very slowly move into a crouched position and do a 360-degree area check. They are approximately twelve feet apart, and after checking the area end up looking at each other. They are equipped with com gear, but use arm and hand signals to communicate in case the enemy is very close.

Both men agree they should move back the way they came and approach from another angle. They slowly stand, turn and start to move back the way they came, when the area the sneeze came from erupts with gunfire.

The two men hit the ground and start crawling as fast as they can. When they find some decent cover, both men start to return fire. At the same time their MP-5s are spitting rounds back at the enemy, the two men are communicating.

"Is this another setup, or did we stumble onto a security post?" Jar Head inquires.

"I think it's a little too much fire power for a security post," answers Doggie.

"Agreed," says Jar Head, "let's fall back. If they follow, we will know for sure."

"On the count of three," Doggie suggests.

"One, two, three," Doggie says into the com unit and both men start firing their MP-5s on full automatic. With that many rounds coming in your direction a person tends to keep his head down until the shooting subsides. With the accuracy of the incoming rounds, only the foolhardy raise up to return fire-and they don't live to repeat the act.

When their magazines are empty, the two turn and make a hasty retreat before the opposition starts firing again. Within seconds the two men blend into the area and almost disappear from view.

As they move quickly back toward the beach area, they hear commands being given in Spanish and realize there is a good chance they would be taking a dirt nap right about now if that person hadn't sneezed.

The enemy is still giving chase as Doggie and Jar Head get close to the beach, and are still in pursuit three miles later.

"These dickheads aren't giving up," Jar Head observes.

"We'll have to pass through the primary extraction point and get picked up at the secondary," Doggie recommends as they approach the planned extraction point.

"If they ever give up the chase," replies Jar Head

As the two men pass through the extraction point they are greeted by the sounds of gunfire in front of them. One of the rounds finds its way to Jar Head's right thigh, and another hits the inside of Doggie's left leg; both men go down. *You alright?* both men inquire at the same instant, and both answer *yes*.

"The tree by the beach," Doggie yells, and both men crawl as fast as they can to get behind it.

The leader of the ambush group, hoping to capitalize on what he thinks is his advantage, commands his men to stand up and charge. He soon changes his mind when three of his men fall dead after taking no more than five steps. He quickly orders his men back into their positions.

"That's why those others kept pursuing us," Doggie exclaims, "like driving a prey to the hunters."

"Well, that removes any doubt about a traitor in Washington," Jar Head exclaims as he fires a burst from his MP-5.

"Well, I guess this will be home for awhile," Doggie announces as both men remove their packs and dig out their first aid kits. They are lucky: both wounds turn out to be flesh wounds. A half-dozen 4x4 pads over the wounds, some tape to hold them in place, and they are back in business.

"The group that was following should be here soon; I better get on the radio to Jack and fill him in on the situation," Jar Head suggests.

"We should break out the grenades and get them ready, too," adds Doggie, and both men once again dig into their packs and produce the hand grenades they brought along.

"And they bust on us for bringing this type of stuff," Jar Head comments.

"What do they know?" Doggie replies, firing another burst from his MP-5.

Jar Head retrieves a small but powerful two-way radio from his pack, and is in the process of contacting com center back at the airstrip. Not knowing how long it will be before another attack would come Jar Head makes it short, sweet and to the point. He then joins Doggie, who is in the process of straightening out the pins on the hand grenades. This will make them easier to pull out before they throw them.

After some time passes, Jar Head wonders, "What is holding up that other group?"

Doggie looks at Jar Head and asks, "Who are you? It's nice the way it is. We shoot once in a while, and they stay over there. Why do you want to change things? You have no patience," continues Doggie.

"If I wanted Patients, I would have been a Doctor," quips Jar Head.

***

At the airstrip, Jack and the four men from the helicopter are going over contingency plans for the extraction when an operator from the com shack rushes into the room.

"Trouble, sir," he informs Jack. "Once Jar Head made contact with us, he bypassed protocol and sent this message in the clear: *Definitely a traitor in Washington, stop. Barely avoided ambush at warehouse, stop. Was pursued to extraction point and ambushed again, stop. Adversaries keeping their distance, but reinforcements should arrive soon, stop. Have a nice day, stop.*"

Before the operator is halfway through the message, the men in the room are already in motion. The pilots and crew take off running out the door on their way to the helicopter. The operator moves to keep up with Jack as he continues reading the message.

Jack's first stop is his office to collect his sidearm and his .45-caliber grease gun. It's an old gun, but Jack says, *When I put something down, I want it to stay down.*

When the operator finishes relaying the message, Jack starts giving orders: "Send an eyes-only message to the DDO containing the radio transmission." Jack is now running out the front door on the way to the helicopter, with the com operator in hot pursuit. "Send the boat out in case we run out of gas on the way back," he yells. "We may be at the extraction point for a long time. That's it."

"Good luck, sir," the operator yells as he stops running with Jack, turns and starts running back to the com shack.

When he gets to the helicopter the rotors are spinning so fast it looks as though the craft is going to leap into the air, with or without the pilots' okay. Jack gets to the door and jumps aboard. Knowing what is going to happen next the two crewmen hook their arms under Jack's armpits. When the pilot sees Jack jump aboard, he immediately puts the craft into motion. The helicopter takes off in a forward direction, picking up speed and altitude quickly. When the craft is barely high enough, the pilot executes a hard turn to the right, and Jack is suddenly happy the two crewmen have a grip on him as he looks out the side door and sees nothing but runway.

As they return to normal flight, going like a bat out of hell, one of the crewmen informs Jack, "I think we may need the gas boat on the return trip."

"Already underway," Jack replies as he finds a seat, buckles up and puts on a com head set so he can communicate with the pilots and crew.

***

Back at the island, the other group finally arrives and several men assemble to discuss the situation. Doggie is watching them through binoculars, and informs Jar Head it looks like an attack is in the planning. After a little crawling, their adversaries stand up for the charge-just what the two defenders are waiting for. With both men staying low, they open up with withering fire at the center of the charge and work their way to the left and right of the line. While Doggie keeps firing, Jar Head pulls the pin on one of the grenades and throws it as hard as he can. Both men duck down low and put fresh mags into their MP-5s. Seconds after the explosion, the two men come up firing and lay down more withering fire.

Between men falling around them and grenades exploding, the others get intimidated and the charge is broken.

After that it's quiet for some time. Doggie had broken out the night vision gear and is keeping track of the opposition when suddenly he remarks, "We're screwed."

"What?" inquires Jar Head.

"Some guy just showed up with a flame thrower."

"Let me guess," comments Jar Head. "The group will send a lot of rounds our way while he moves in to roast our asses."

"Well, let's take some of them with us," Doggie announces as he removes a roll of adhesive tape from his first-aid kit. While Jar Head is busy with his plan, Doggie wraps tape around each grenade and places it back on the ground. That completed, he again picks up the first grenade and removes the pin. If the spoon on the grenade is not held in place, it will fly off, and seconds later the grenade will explode. In this case the spoon is held in place by the tape. Doggie throws the grenade out in front of their position and continues the process with the remaining grenades. Ten minutes later, everything is still quiet.

"When they told me at the Agency I would be involved with some of the hot spots around the world, this is not what I had in mind," says Jar Head.

"Well we had a good run," offers Doggie.

"Yeah, we can't complain," Jar Head agrees. "I wonder if we'll go to Heaven, or to Hell?"

A second after the question is asked, gunfire erupts and rounds starting hitting all around Jar Head and Doggie's position.

"It looks like we're about to find out," Doggie exclaims, then looks at Jar Head and says, "See you later."

"Not if I see you first," Jar Head quips, then extends his hand. The two men shake hands good bye, then get back to the business at hand.

The high volume of rounds coming in are doing what they are supposed to do. The two defenders can't rise up long enough to locate the man they know is crawling towards their position, and it isn't long before the man with the flame thrower is close enough for his assault. Now he has to get into position and light the flame inside the nozzle of the thrower, and when he squeezes the trigger, fuel under pressure in two tanks he carries on his back will flow down a hose on its journey to the flame in the nozzle. It will then be ignited, and the burning fuel is launched to burn anything in its path.

The man slowly gets up, and with his right knee on the ground and his left foot on the ground in front, he leans forward.

After selecting his first target he squeezes the front trigger to light the match in the nozzle, then he squeezes the back trigger with his right hand and flame streams towards Doggie and Jar Head's defensive position. The base of the tree is immediately engulfed in fire. The site resembles firefighting in reverse: Instead of water putting out a fire, it's fire starting a fire. After the initial burst, the flame thrower operator stands and moves closer to his target, squeezing off a few more short bursts.

Not all of the burning fuel reaches its destination when using a flame thrower. Small amounts of the fuel lose their forward momentum and fall to the ground, creating little pockets of fire that burn for a short period of time.

At this point, the tree and the surrounding area are already an inferno. As the man moves to get closer, his assistant advises against it, but the flame thrower operator says, "I am going to make sure there are no remains of these Americans." and continues walking forward.

When he is satisfied with the distance, he leans forward and again squeezes the trigger.

The noise and spectacle of the flame thrower obscures the sound of a spoon flying off one of the hand grenades Doggie had deposited in front of their position. A small bit of flame had landed close enough to a grenade to set the adhesive tape on fire, and a short time later the tape can no longer hold the spoon in place.

The man has just started another burst when the grenade explodes, rupturing one of the fuel tanks and spinning the man around to his left, spraying his assistant and the two other men with flame. When the ruptured tank comes in contact with the small flames burning on the ground, it erupts into an inferno. Two of the men that are consumed in flames are running towards the beach and the ocean, but are shot by their own men as an act of mercy.

Before the attackers can regroup, two more grenades explode. Between exploding grenades and rounds cooking off that Jar Head had thrown in front of their position, the hostiles decides to retire. There may be grenades on the verge of exploding...and who knows what other tricks these Americans have in place.

The main man is present, and tells the men to collect the wounded and head back to the estate. These Americans are dead, and there is no reason for losing additional men. As his men are leaving, the boss looks at the burning tree and says out loud, "That's what will happen to any American dog that comes to my island," then spits on the ground and turns to join his men.

***

It is a moonless night as the helicopter finally reaches the island, and all are wearing night-vision gear. Not being able to raise Jar Head and Doggie on their com units, the copter moves in cautiously as it approaches the extraction point. Moving a little further down the beach, the craft lands; Jack and one of the crewmen jump out to recon the area while the copter hovers, with the door gunner ready to engage any unfriendlies. The tree is a smoldering stump as Jack and the crewman approach the site. They quickly survey the area and discover two badly charred backpacks that probably belonged to

Doggie and Jar Head.

"What's it look like down there?" one of the pilots inquires.

"It's isn't pretty," Jack informs him. "A lot of charred bodies."

The two men are still looking around when they hear the sound of a spoon flying off a grenade.

"Hit the deck!" yells Jack, and both men dive for cover. When the grenade explodes it shakes the ground the two are laying on. The copter immediately moves in closer and the door gunner scans the area for anything that moves, but nothing happens. "We'd better come back during the day so we can get a better idea of what we are looking at," Jack advises. "We'll collect the backpacks, then we all will beat the bush a little before we move further down the beach for pickup."

Once back by the packs, Jack gives the order and all open fire. After spraying the area, Jack and his partner pick up the packs and move down the beach while the door gunner continues beating up the brush.

Fifty-five seconds later, Jack and the crewman are throwing the backpacks onto the helicopter, and climbing aboard themselves. The copter stays low as it races down the beach, then out to sea. Halfway back to the airstrip the adrenaline has stopped pumping, and an unspoken sadness settles over the craft.

The next morning, Jack is in the middle of briefing the pilots, the crew and the additional manpower that will be going to the island this morning, when a man from the com unit enters the room.

"Flash traffic, sir," he says, holding out a folded piece of paper. Jack takes the paper and quickly reads it. "Bullshit," he exclaims, then tells the men to review the map until he returns from the com shack.

Ten minutes later Jack comes back into the room and flops into a chair, still holding the piece of paper in his left hand.

"Washington ordered us to stand down," Jack informs the others.

"Why?" one of the pilots inquires.

"Politics again," Jack replies. "The Ambassador to Nicaragua is telling Washington that 'things are being disrupted, and prior to last night's incident everything was running smoothly.'"

"Did anyone stop to wonder how an incident on an island off the coast of Nicaragua, in the middle of the night, got reported to Washington so quickly they were able to make a decision by six a.m. the same morning?" asks the pilot.

"You know how that goes," Jack starts his reply. "It depends on the current Administration. Some Administrations put in people that think and wonder, and others don't." After a pause, Jack adds, "It looks like the bad people are real happy with this Administration."

There is something that only he and the senior com operator know. Due to the conversation they had with Doggie and Jar Head when they first arrived about the possibility of a traitor in Washington, he did not include in his message to Langley that they had already made a trip to the island the night before.

He just included the transmission sent by Jar Head, and stated that he would be leaving for the island in the morning. Jack is an avid fly fisherman, and is casting out his line hoping the traitor would try to head off the morning visit, and it looks like he has something on his line. It's easy to disclaim the truth when it is just radio communications with no eye's on confirmation to back up your claims.

Before Jack returned to the group, he placed a call to Gert and requested a face-to-face in Washington with Swabbie.

Jack and the others liked Doggie and Jar Head very much and will miss them, but they will always remember their smiling faces, and the exciting projects they shared together.

CHAPTER TWELVE

E verything is starting to move too fast, and the DDO puts a hold on any additional action on the matter. He then makes a call to apologize for terminating the meetings. His counterpart in the UK completely understands, and wishes him well with this latest flap.

The cruise ship is in port when Swabbie receives a message from Gert. He and Anne immediately make arrangements to fly back to Washington.

As a plane from the Caribbean and another from London make their way to Washington, D.C., three people on those planes sit in complete silence, remembering their friends: the many experiences, the good times in and outside the Agency. Their thoughts also include Jessie and Mims, and how they are going to tell them about what has happened. Both women knew the dangers and risks their men faced in the professions they had chosen, but tried not to dwell on the matter.

Swabbie and Dunn have additional thoughts. This is not the first time they've lost friends during action in the field, but those times were different. Those men and women had a chance. They were not set up by a traitor in their own organization. This fact will not be forgotten, and the person or persons will pay for their treachery that has slaughtered their friends and others.

***

One month passes, and things have not been pleasant at the Agency. It has been discovered that the main man on the island has an associate that also happens to be a member of the Cuban government.

That explains how information was passed to the main man on the island so he could ambush Doggie and Jar Head. Even with these new revelations, the State Department holds fast to its position on the area and the Administration backs them.

Dunn and Swabbie are having a hard time keeping Bean and Blue Jay in check. They want to finish the job their mentors started and several flare-ups have occurred between the four. The atmosphere is very tense.

Dunn and Swabbie are facing a dilemma. They both want to give

Bean and Blue Jay the go-ahead, but orders from above prevent it.

Swabbie held a meeting with Jack at a Washington restaurant, and Jack told him everything about his conversations with Jar Head and Doggie, from when they first arrived to the visit he made to the island.

The next morning, Swabbie is in Dunn's office informing him about the meeting, and what Jack had told him.

When Swabbie finishes, Dunn announces, "We have to get whoever is responsible for these betrayals. Not just because two of our friends have been killed, but for all the others in the past and any future agents that may be terminated."

At the end of their meeting, both men agree not to share the information about Jack's trip to the island. The fact that a Cuban official is involved, and probably supplied the information that allowed both this and the prior ambush to take place, will also not be shared. If Bean and Blue Jay hear it from a reliable source, there will be no holding them back.

***

Blue Jay and Bean have been doing more than just arguing with their bosses for the past two weeks. They have been gathering information and tracing Doggie and Jar Head's movements, from the time the general called to their trip to Honduras.

Information is not easy to get, partly due to the DDO labeling it eyes-only, need-to-know, and anything else he can think of to keep the information from getting to them. Dunn needs time to uncover the traitor, and then maybe things will change and the project will be allowed to reactivate.

***

Two weeks later, since the State Department and the Administration forbid any visits back on the island to gather remains, a private memorial is held for Jar Head and Doggie. Everyone is solemn as clergy and friends say nice words about the two men. Mims and Jessie hold up well at first, but finally break down and are consoled by Anne and Swabbie.

Bean and Blue Jay seem to be dealing with the situation. Maybe that weeks' vacation did them some good. Outside of an occasional watery eye, they are doing well and seem to be focused on what the speakers have to say. They merely sit with no emotion showing on their suntanned faces: *the sun is hot in Honduras.*

Dunn has seen this look on the faces of other men in years past, and knows what it means. He will have to talk with them tomorrow.

When the services are through, all in attendance go to pay their respects to Mims and Jessie.

Blue Jay and Bean drift to the area where flowers have been arranged for the service, and each man removes two roses and places the ends of the stems into little water reservoirs they had obtained from the florist when they ordered flowers. They wait until all have paid their respects to the two ladies, and then approach them. Blue Jay hands one of the roses to Mims and keeps the other, while Bean does the same with Jessie. Both women are touched by the gesture, stand and give the young men a kiss on the cheek before they are escorted to a waiting limo, then onto an after-service brunch.

***

It is 10 a.m. the following morning, and Dunn has summoned Bean and Blue Jay to his office. Swabbie is already in attendance when they arrive, so they join the two men at the conference table.

"I want to talk with you two to see how you are dealing with the losses we have suffered."

"We're doing okay," answers Blue Jay.

"Yes, we are," adds Bean, "we were trained by the best."

"I hope you aren't planning any little project on your own," inquires Dunn.

"Not that I know of," offers Bean.

"Don't give me that shit," replies Dunn. "I saw that look on both your faces yesterday at the service, and I know what it means."

"So you're telling us that you're now eating Gypsy shit and telling fortunes?" inquires Blue Jay, sending Dunn into orbit. An hour later, Dunn is starting to lose his voice and the two are still claiming innocence. After a final warning, Dunn dismisses the two. When they have left the office Dunn asks Swabbie, "What do you think?"

"I don't know," answers Swabbie.

"Don't give me that," Dunn snaps. "What do you think?"

"I think some people better put their heads down between their legs and kiss their asses goodbye," answers Swabbie.

"I am afraid I have to agree with you," Dunn replies as he starts pondering the statement.

CHAPTER THIRTEEN

H aving already touched base with the Section Chief in the Special OPS unit and Jack in Honduras, things have been put into place for Bean and Blue Jay's planned visit to the island of Cayos. After that visit, they will deal with the Cuban.

Two days have passed since the memorial services and the new Dynamic Duo are in the process of leaving Swabbie's office when he asks a question out of the blue: "So, when are you planning to leave for Cayos?"

"I wasn't aware that project was reactivated," Blue Jay replies without hesitation.

"Does that mean we have a go on the project?"

inquires Bean enthusiastically.

"No," replies Swabbie, "I'm just checking."

Blue Jay is last to leave the office, and as he closes the door behind him mumbles, "Nice try, *dick.*"

"Tell me about it," Bean replies in a low voice.

When Bean and Blue Jay stop to chat with Gert, they are both surprised when she offers to buy them a cup of coffee at the cafeteria. Both men agree and accompany her. After getting her coffee, Gert heads for an empty table surrounded by other empty tables. Once everyone is seated Gert starts the conversation with small talk. When the conversation moves on to Jar Head and Doggie, Gert goes into her purse, produces a small stack of tissues and puts them on the table. She then removes the first one and blows her nose.

The talk continues and Gert reaches for another tissue. When she removes the second tissue it reveals the words *Dunn and Swabbie getting close to your plan* printed on the third tissue.

The two immediately see the words, and Gert removes the tissue, blows her nose on it and will flush it later in the ladies' room.

Not knowing Gert's motives, Bean and Blue Jay play dumb and Gert continues using the Jar Head-Doggie conversation as a cover for the real subject, Dunn and Swabbie.

"They were around the Intelligence game for a lot of years," Gert starts. "They would bend the rules a little, but if a direct order came down from the top they would obey. They both had good instincts, and if they had a strong feeling about something, they were relentless."

Realizing what Gert is doing, Blue Jay poses a question: "We both picked up on that. What was the shortest amount of time it ever took them to resolve one of their strong feelings?"

Gert stops and pretends she is thinking as she again wipes her nose with the tissue. "I would say one, maybe two days," she answers.

"They were good," adds Bean.

"Yes, they were," Gert adds, "and that time no one was giving up any information on the matter."

Gert then started talking about Mims and Jessie, and the conversation changed back to Doggie and Jar Head.

***

Thirty minutes later, Blue Jay and Bean have escorted Gert back to her desk, thanked her for the coffee (information) and are walking slowly down the hall thinking about what Gert had said. The three main facts are: *Dunn and Swabbie are hot on their trail; about two days max from discovering our plan;* and *the plan is still intact because no one is talking.*

When they get to the parking lot, Blue Jay breaks the silence with, "Bean, what do you have planned for tomorrow?"

"Same old, same old," replies Bean.

"Want to go deep-sea fishing?" asks Blue Jay. "I know of a place where we can rent a boat. We'll stock it with food and booze, leave real early in the morning and stay out for a few days."

"Won't the management get a little peeved if we don't show up for work?" inquires Bean.

"What difference does it make?" replies Blue Jay.

"They won't let us do what we came here for, so we may as well go fishing."

"You and this problem with management. When will it end?" Bean inquires with mock concern.

"It's what I do," laughs Blue Jay as both men open the car doors and get in.

As the Ford Crown Victoria and its two passengers drive past the main gate at CIA headquarters, a man enters the DDO's office and hands him a piece of paper. Dunn takes the paper, quickly reads it and says, "Good, being out on the ocean for a few days may clear their minds, and it will definitely keep them off of mine. That long-range listening device works pretty good," Dunn approves, then returns to the business at hand.

As the man turns to leave, Dunn orders, "Send someone to make sure their fishing boat gets launched."

***

At 1 a.m. the next morning, the Ford is speeding down Route 50 towards the Chesapeake Bay. The car is moving a little slow for Blue Jay's liking, but they don't want to lose the Agency vehicles that are tailing them to the fishing boat.

Dunn and Swabbie aren't the only ones that are good at this Intelligence stuff.

Two hours later, a boat has been rented. The food and booze have been unloaded from the Ford and put onto the boat, and while Bean puts the car in long-term parking, Blue Jay fires up the boat's engines for a last-minute check.

When Bean returns to the dock, he casts off all of the boat's mooring lines, goes aboard, and pushes the craft away from the dock. With that done, Blue Jay cycles up the engines and the boat moves slowly away from the dock. With Blue Jay in charge of the boat, Bean goes below, breaks out a spotter scope, returns to just below deck level and focuses in on the dock area. After a few minutes, several men appear on the dock, have a brief conversation, and depart.

Bean leaves his position for a few seconds then returns with night-vision gear and sweeps the area, looking for boats with or without their running lights on, finding none.

"Looks like no one is following," he informs his partner.

"Good," a relieved Blue Jay replies as the boat picks up speed. "It would have taken up too much time to lose them."

The boat is going full speed, and gives the impression it is going to leave the bay and head for the open sea, when Blue Jay cycles down the engines a little. It is still dark, and both men are wearing night-vision gear. Blue Jay steers the boat towards shore and cycles the engine down again.

"You're right on the money," announces Bean as he uses his arm and hand to point to a location on shore. Blue Jay again cycles down the engines and the craft moves slowly towards an old abandoned shack that extends out over the water. Wouldn't want to live there, but it's good enough to hide a boat. Having sides and a roof, even spy in the sky will not be able to locate it.

As the boat slowly enters the shack, the Chief appears and Bean throws him a mooring line. He catches it and secures it to the structure. Blue Jay cuts the engines, and as Bean and the Chief secure a second line, Blue Jay jumps off the other side of the boat and moves to close the right side of the shakes door. Bean does the same for the left door.

"Do you still want in on this project?" Blue Jay asks the Chief one last time.

"Do I still want in?" snaps the Chief. "Does a fish fart? You know, the last time I saw your fathers, I told them you were going to be trouble."

"What did they say?" Bean asks.

"They said, 'We can only hope'," the Chief chuckles. "Now, let's get rolling."

The three men get into a black 4X4, and after navigating some secondary roads they are on Route 50 heading back towards Washington. Once they reach the Washington beltway they will follow it to Andrews Air Force Base and a waiting business jet.

CHAPTER FOURTEEN

J ack is waiting when the business jet from Andrews comes to a stop in front of the main building. As Bean and Blue Jay deplane, Jack inquires, "Have a good flight?"

"Yes, and got some sack time," Bean replies.

"Good," Jack approves, "with the schedule you two have set up for yourselves, you should get sleep whenever you can."

The first stop is the armory, where Blue Jay and Bean change from civilian clothes into camouflage utilities and boots. Then they load up their backpacks with high energy food packets, water, explosives, additional ammunition and other assorted goodies.

Next are the weapons. Both men will carry a 9mm Beretta sidearm, a 9mm MP-5 automatic weapon with silencer and a Randal-made fighting knife. Once the men have all of their gear, they take some loaded magazines for their weapons and put a few extra in their packs. Then both men pick up their gear, grab a kill suit and follow Jack to the briefing room.

Already knowing the pilots and crew from their visit ten days ago, no formal introductions are necessary.

"Nothing has changed much since the briefings you had the first time you were here," Jack offers.

"We would like to change the insertion point," Blue Jay says. "The one we selected when we were here last time is too close to the area where the action took place. As part of this project, we wanted to check out the area, but our research shows the main man on the island is watching it, and our State Department is watching it, so our suggestion is to land about four miles up the beach on the other side of the main man's villa."

"We can follow the beach down towards the villa, and when we are close enough, angle in towards the warehouse, then move on to the villa," Bean adds. Bean and Blue Jay notice a silence has come over the group, and look up from the map at the others.

"Sorry," Jack says, "we were just remembering. Those other two guys had the same plan when they approached from the other side of the villa."

"Well, it's not much of a plan," Bean confesses. "But they always told us, 'keep it simple, stupid'."

"That sounds like something they would say," Jack says, and all of the others smile and agree.

An hour later, Jack and the others are at the helicopter pad and five minutes later the rotors pick up speed in preparation for liftoff. Jack will be going along for this one. If fuel becomes a problem the gas boat will come into play.

***

The sun is setting when the helicopter is halfway to the insertion point. It is a beautiful, peaceful site and would be enjoyed by all if they were not headed into harm's way.

It is dark when the craft is ten miles from the insertion point, and the copter drops down low and almost skims the water. Blue Jay and Bean have put on their packs, checked their weapons and are ready to go. Minutes later, the craft reduces speed and is approaching the spot. When the copter comes to a full stop and hovers inches over the beach, Bean and Blue Jay jump out and get out of the open. The instant the two passengers are off the craft, it proceeds twenty yards further down the beach comes to a halt, turns back out to sea and moves off the beach.

The copter will not hover over the horizon this time. It will proceed to an area along the coast of the island where the terrain is so rough you need a boat or helicopter to get to the beach. After landing, they will wait for the pickup call from the two men.

Blue Jay and Bean waste no time. They immediately move thirty yards inland, and then in the direction of their objective. Under normal circumstances they would take it slower, maybe make it a two-day project, blow up the warehouse and take out the main man at a distance. But these are not normal circumstances. After this, they have to move on the Cuban before Dunn and Swabbie can stop them.

Three hours later, Bean and Blue Jay are at the warehouse surveying the area. Other than the two guards shooting the shit at the entrance, no other security can be seen. It seems the main man thinks that since the U.S. State Department put out the word about Nicaragua, no one will come calling. After a few more seconds of looking, the two men move towards the rear of the warehouse, cut the padlock and enter. Blue Jay will place incendiary devices in an area of the warehouse to make it look like a fire caused by spontaneous combustion, while Bean plants high explosives under explosives already stacked in the warehouse. Bean joins Blue Jay just as he finishes rearranging things to give the fire fuel when the incendiaries ignite.

Packing material from some of the open boxes are placed behind a 50-gallon oil drum. He then removes a small roll of electrical tape, tears off a piece and places it at the bottom of the oil drum. He removes his knife from its scabbard, places the point in the middle of the tape and while holding the knife in place with his left hand, strikes the end of the knife handle with his right and the blade punctures the barrel *They make them good at Randal,* he thinks. With oil slowly oozing out of the barrel, Blue Jay picks up the incendiary device, sets the timer for 30 minutes and shows Bean, who shakes his head in approval. Blue Jay then places it on some packing and covers it with additional packing. That completed, the two quietly leave the warehouse and move towards the Villa.

The fire gets a good start before it's discovered and the alarm sounds. Even the oil has reached its kindling temperature and is contributing to the blaze as a group of men appear from the main house at the villa.

The blaze at the warehouse can be seen over the trees, and when the main man sees his profits going up in flames, he immediately orders his men to go fight the fire. After a quick conversation, all but six of his security force at the villa pile into vehicles and leave to fight the fire.

When the vehicles are out of the area, Bean and Blue Jay start to move in closer to the men at the villa, who are still looking in the direction of the blaze.

The plan seems to be working out well, until one of the security men says something into the main man's ear…it looks like the small party will be moving inside.

Seeing what is happening, Bean quickly removes a remote detonator from his left breast pocket, pulls up its small antenna, and arms the detonator. After looking to make sure Blue Jay is ready, he presses the button and a large explosion erupts at the warehouse. The noise from the explosion is still in the air when Bean and Blue Jay start firing their MP-5s, taking down the two men at the left and right ends of the group. Caught off-guard, the security men react slower than they normally would, and two more go down. The remaining two return fire as they push the main man towards the open door of the house. Blue Jay and Bean are moving quickly towards the house and are about to release another burst when they come under fire themselves.

Two men that were probably sleeping through it all and were awakened by the explosions are firing their automatic weapons at them. Bean and Blue Jay immediately swing to the right and return fire, taking both men out of action, but when they turn back to the primary target, he has disappeared into the house with his security men.

The two men replace their magazines with fresh ones and move towards the house. Positioning themselves on either side of the front door, Bean takes a quick look inside, then ducks back to his original position. At the same time Blue Jay is doing the same at the window to his right. Bean looks at Blue Jay and says, "We don't have time for this."

"No shit!" replies Blue Jay as he produces a hand grenade.

"The explosion may bring unwanted people," comments Bean.

"Not if we don't pull the pin," whispers Blue Jay, and Bean understands immediately.

"Here," says Blue Jay as he tosses the grenade to Bean, "from that side you can use your right hand to throw it."

Bean gets into position, then throws the grenade in the doorway as hard as he can and hollers "Fire in the hole!" for good measure.

The man hiding on the stairway can see the grenade as it bounces around the foyer and knows he has only seconds to get away, but is put down by Blue Jay as he tries to run up the stairs.

The two men move inside, and Blue Jay collects his grenade. They check the front room, but it is empty. As they approach the second room a nervous main man opens fire prematurely, and after brief return fire from Blue Jay and Bean, the main man and his remaining security are both dead.

Bean walks over and stands alongside the main man's body, reaches into the left lower pocket of his camouflaged utilities and produces a white rose that has been slightly singed by flame. After removing its stem from a tiny reservoir, he throws the flower on the floor next to the body. After a few seconds' pause, the two are again on the move and heading for the back of the house. Once outside and halfway across the courtyard, a vehicle full of security men come around the corner of the building.

"Ah, shit," Bean exclaims as he turns and fires at the men in the 4X4.

Blue Jay is firing with one hand and retrieving the grenade with the other as he and Bean fall to the ground to avoid incoming fire. Blue Jay pulls the pin on the grenade and releases the lever. When the spoon is released, it gives off a telltale sound, and after a pause Blue Jay throws it at the 4X4. A few seconds later, the grenade explodes and the vehicle jumps off the ground in a ball of flame. Bean and Blue Jay are on their feet, charging and firing as they go until they have eliminated the opposition. Two minutes later, they are away from the villa and have melted into the underbrush.

***

It is very quiet where the helicopter is waiting until the radio starts to crackle. After confirming they want to be picked up at the primary point, the rotors start turning and the copter gets underway. The pickup is on the beach, two miles from the villa, and will be done on the move. Blue Jay and Bean, wearing night-vision gear, can see the copter approaching and move onto the beach. The pilots spot their pickups and reduce speed. As they get to the men, the copter keeps moving slowly forward. Bean and Blue Jay move with the craft and, one at a time, with the help of the crew members, manage to get aboard. When the second man is on board the craft picks up speed, then banks to the left and heads out to sea. After the two have removed their backpacks and put on the helicopter's com head sets, a voice inquires, "Did you get it done?"

"We got it done."

CHAPTER FIFTEEN

A fter the helicopter touches down at the airstrip, Blue Jay and Bean go to the armory then to the briefing room and find Jack talking with the two pilots of the business jet.

"We have to make some changes; the Cuban is on the move," Jack informs the two men as they enter the room.

"Where is he now?" Blue Jay inquires.

"We thought he was heading back to Cuba, but it looks like he decided to stop in Jamaica on the way home," Jack answers. "Probably to touch base with some friends of Cuba."

"I guess we have to cancel the plan for him," Bean remarks.

"I am working on an alternate plan," Jack informs them. "You two get some sleep, and I'll wake you when I have it worked out."

Bean and Blue Jay are too tired to argue, and head for some sack time.

At 6 a.m., Jack is running his plan past Blue Jay and Bean.

"I have been in touch with a friend of mine that works for British Intelligence and is stationed in Jamaica," Jack begins. "He informs me the Cuban did arrive yesterday morning, and that he is staying at a local resort. During the day, it's golf; at night he meets in his suite with people that have close ties with Cuba."

"Would he share information with us about the Cuban's movements?" asks Bean.

"Better than that," Jack answers quickly. "He thinks we can do each other a service, but I'll let him fill you in. If you like my plan, the business jet will take you over to Montego Bay. You will rent a car, follow the directions I will give you and meet with him. What do you think?" inquires Jack.

"We don't have a plan for the Jamaica location," Blue Jay reminds everyone.

"That will be covered when you contact the Brit," Jack replies. "If you don't like what he has to say, the Jet will take you back to the U.S."

The two men ponder the alternatives, and then both agree to go for the meeting. If they don't get him on this trip, they may never get another chance.

After the two men have cleaned up and changed back into civvies, they go to see Jack for the directions.

Per Bean and Blue Jay's request, all pilots and crew members are present. "We want to thank all of you for your help with this project," Blue Jay says. "We know you all put your necks on the line.

"We also want to thank you for helping Doggie and Jar Head on their projects," Bean adds.

"No problem," one of the crewmen replies out loud, "just make sure you get it done. If we all get caught, we don't want to have done all this for nothing."

"One down, and one to go," confirms Jack.

"No pressure," says Bean.

"Yeah, I know," replies Blue Jay. "Who was that crewman anyway?"

The serious mood is broken, and the group laughs as they all leave the room and escort the two men to the airstrip and the plane.

After the pilots and crew get the plane ready for takeoff, Blue Jay and Bean thank Jack and the others again, bid them farewell and board the plane.

The plane taxies for takeoff, and within five minutes the jet is moving down the runway like a big-ass bird.

Just before it reaches the place where Jack and others are standing, the nose of the jet starts to rise, and by the time they pass the group the plane is airborne. The men in the plane and on the ground exchange a final wave goodbye as the plane continues its climb into the sky.

***

It is 1 p.m. when the two men are leaving the airport grounds. Bean is behind the wheel; Blue Jay is looking at the map and getting oriented.

"We have to get up that hill," Blue Jay instructs as he points to a big hill a short distance from the airport gate.

"How far up?" asks Bean.

"Do you see those red roof houses?" Blue Jay points to the top of the hill.

"Yeah," answers Bean.

"Well, its past them," he confirms.

"Like this car is going to make it," Bean muses.

"I'm more worried about brakes and the trip down," Blue Jay smiles.

A short time later they are at the top of the hill and coming to a halt in front of a red-roofed house. They get out and proceed to the door.

On the second series of knocks, the door swings open and a British gentlemen asks, "May I help you?"

Blue Jay says the word Jack gave them, and the man in the doorway replies with the counter.

"Come in," the Brit insists. "How is Jack? We communicate, but I haven't seen him for about two years."

"Doing very well," Bean answers. "He is a good man."

"Yes, he is," agrees the Brit. "After the initial communication with Jack about your project, I started wondering if we might do each other a service. Let's go into the clean room and discuss it," he continues, and leads them down a series of steps and into an underground cellar. "I believe your situation is, you want the Cuban, but your higher-ups say no."

Blue Jay acknowledges with a head shake.

"Well, I am afraid we are in the same situation," the Brit continues. "We have been using a man for years to get information and the like, but lately some of our chaps have gone missing. Long story short, we traced it back to the man we have been using. We pay him very well, but he got greedy and is playing both sides. We wanted to settle the score, but home office said no."

"We know the feeling," Bean says.

"If we help you get in and out of the resort, and anything else you require to get at the Cuban, do you think you could get our man as well?"

"Do you have pictures of the resort?" inquires Blue Jay.

"And a picture of your man," adds Bean.

"Jolly good," the Brit exclaims as he stands to go get the requested photos. As he returns he suggests, "We had a plan in place and ready to go until we were put on hold. You are welcome to use it, but with such a short time frame I think it would be easier to follow your own plan than learn the plan we have in place." Blue Jay and Bean agree, and can see why Jack and the Brit are friends. Both are quick-minded and good people.

The Brits had done their homework on the resort: they have photos from every angle in and outside of the resort and a video of the grounds, the lobby, one of the floors and a view from one of the balconies.

After two hours of viewing the material and asking questions, the Brit suggests a tea break, and ten minutes later the three men are sitting on the patio that faces the airport.

"This is a good vantage point," offers Bean.

"Quite so," answers the Brit, "with that telescope in there, I can see any plane or person coming, going, landing or taking off."

"It is a beautiful place to be stationed," Blue Jay comments as he looks down towards the sea and the beaches in the distance.

"It was almost shut down after the Cold War supposedly ended, but then this business with Cuba started up again and we got a reprieve," the Brit offers.

"What is your opinion on Cuba?" Bean asks.

"My personal opinion is that the only thing keeping them in check is a lack of funds to export their brand of communism to the Caribbean, Central America, South America, and the like. People are quick to forget when Castro was supported by the Russians. He had troops in Nicaragua and Angola, and was involved in things the general public didn't know about. Even now, he is trying to link up with other dictators to get something started."

"I agree with you," Bean replies. "Some people in this world only care about dollars, and not about the consequences of their actions, until things get out of hand or they create something they can't control anymore."

"Then they cry to our government for help," Blue Jay comments.

"Quite so," says the Brit. "More tea?" he offers, seeing he has two new friends with the same outlook.

The discussion continues for another thirty minutes, then Blue Jay and Bean returned to the photos while the Brit performs some of his daily duties. An hour later, he joins the other two and inquires, "You chaps have any additional questions?"

"Yes," Bean answers quickly. "Can you get us some scuba gear? We will enter the resort via the beach area."

"We can do better than that," the Brit smiles. "We have scuba and a few two-man underwater sleds. Our chaps can give you a ride to and from the resort. It is unfortunate, but getting you in and out without being detected will be the extent of our support, due to our home office situation."

"Understood, and no problem," answers Bean. "You are being extremely helpful."

"We have another request, but due to the time factor we'll understand if you can't supply them." states Blue Jay. "Do you have a way to acquire two Russian-made pistols, possibly equipped with silencers?"

In response, the Brit starts to laugh.

"I don't blame you," Blue Jay responds. "I would laugh too if someone ask me for something like that on such short notice."

"Not at all," the Brit waves off Blue Jay's remarks. "When Jack and I were in Nicaragua, we collected a few weapons from our

Russian-supplied adversaries. I may have something that meets your requirement."

The Brit stands and motions for the others to follow. He walks across the small room, opens a door and enters a smaller room, then proceeds to the far corner where a sump pump is installed. The Brit pulls up on the sump pump float, and the water is pumped up a hose and out of the house.

"You get water this high up the hill?" inquires Bean.

"Not a drop," answers the Brit, "I keep water in it for show."

When the water is pumped out, the Brit requests Bean to remove the pump. That done, he bends down and twists the bucket-type device the pump was sitting in to the right, and then removes it from the hole, revealing a burlap bag. Blue Jay quickly reaches down and retrieves it, and all return to the other room.

Inside the burlap bag is another heavy plastic bag containing several Russian-made pistols, along with three silencers.

"I am afraid they will require a bit of cleaning,"

says the Brit. "I had to keep them well-lubricated due to storing them in the hole."

"No problem," Blue Jay assures the Brit. "I see you have cleaning gear right here in the bag."

"I'll let you to it, then," the Brit says. "I'll go check on the locations of our friends at the resort."

An hour later, the Brit returns just as Bean is putting the last few rounds into the magazine of a third pistol they have decided to take with them.

"Do you mind if we take this third weapon as well?" asks Bean.

"Not at all," exclaims the Brit, then he sits down to brief the two on the locations of the men at the resort. The briefing then turns to their escape route, and an alternative route if the primary can't be used.

"Your primary escape route will be the same way you arrived. After dropping you off, my lads will take your scuba gear and the sleds and wait for you offshore. When they see you on the beach, they will move in for pickup. If this route gets cut off, I'm afraid you are in for a bit of a walk," the Brit apologizes. "You will have to exit via the front of the resort and make your way overland to the other side of Montego Bay, and we will have to make other arrangements for pickup."

Bean and Blue Jay are not bothered by the last statement, and are absorbing all of the information like sponges soaking up liquid from a kitchen spill.

When the briefing is done and all questions are answered, the Brit suggests brunch, then on to meet his lads with the scuba gear.

CHAPTER SIXTEEN

I t is early evening, and the resort is jumping. The night's entertainment is located at an outside stage in the pool area. Jamaican music fills the air, and the resort guests are completely enjoying the event.

At the far left end of the beach, the two sleds deposit their passengers on a jetty that extends out into the water. When Blue Jay and Bean's scuba gear are lashed in place, the sleds move off to wait for the extraction.

Blue Jay and Bean had planned this project before they knew the Cuban would be at this resort, and are both wearing solid green suits complete with tight-fitting hoods. Their suits will blend in with the trees and other foliage, but if they get caught in the light with the tan walls of the resorts hotel as a background, it could be trouble.

The two move off the beach and proceed toward the building at the right of the hotel complex. The entertainment is between the hotel's two buildings, and the music echoes all over the complex. Blue Jay and Bean stop and survey the area before moving to the right rear side of the building. Once there, they stop and again survey the area. That done, Blue Jay looks at Bean and gives a thumbs-up, and Bean replies with the same. Another quick look and, keeping low, Blue Jay is moving quickly towards a palm tree at the corner of the building.

Once he reaches his objective he stops and whispers into his com head set: "All clear?" While Bean again checks the grounds and balconies for movement, Blue Jay produces claw-type equipment and straps them to his wrists. He then adjusts the claw device so the back side lays flat against his palms and puts his middle finger all the way through a loop at the other end to hold the claws in place.

Seconds later, Bean gives him the OK and he starts climbing the palm tree to the second-floor balcony, where no inside lights are showing against the curtain. Reaching the balcony, he carefully moves from the tree to the balcony, goes to the right-hand corner and starts to replace the claws with special gloves for his next phase.

"In position," Bean hears in his com unit as he gets ready for his part of the plan. He first removes a rolled-up beach bag that was supplied by the Brit, unrolls it, reaches inside and produces a towel.

Bean then removes his green suit to reveal a pair of shorts and a resort tee shirt. He quickly puts the suit, com gear, and two Russian hand guns into the beach bag, and gets underway to find the man that has been playing both sides, getting both British and his fellow Jamaicans killed in the process.

With the towel around his neck and his beach bag in tow, both bearing the resort monogram, Bean walks around the back perimeter of the hotel looking for his man, but has no luck. *Maybe he is in the front,* Bean thinks to himself. Taking a wide arc to reach the front, Bean stands between the hotel front and the road that passes the resort seventy yards away. As he scans from left to right, he still doesn't see his target-but then he gets lucky. Standing at the far right, in front of the hotel travel office, his man is talking with another hotel employee.

A few minutes pass, and the conversation breaks up and his man enters the hotel lobby. *Just keep walking,* Bean thinks to himself. The man crosses the lobby area and continues out the back door to the pool area. Bean is on his way before the man gets out the door. Watching him from a distance, he waits until the man wanders down past the pool and to the steps leading to the beach. When Bean approaches him, he says the words the Brit told him, so the man will know what he wants.

"What can I do for you, mon?" the man inquires.

"I need some assistance," Bean relays. "I am on my own and I have to take out someone."

"I don't do that sort of ting," the man informs Bean.

"I'll make it well worth your while," says Bean, and produces a stack of bills.

"No, not for me," the man insists, and Bean produces another stack from the beach bag. The man's eyes light up when he sees the second stack; suddenly it's too hard for him to pass up. That money, along with the money from the other side will add up to a big payday. "Okay," the man says, excited about the money, "but I have to go get a gun."

"I have an extra," Bean informs him as he walks down the steps to the beach. After walking along the beach a few yards, Bean put his hand into the bag, hooks the trigger guard with his first finger, produces the Russian-made pistol and hands it to the Jamaican. The man takes the weapon and immediately removes the magazine and checks the rounds. He then puts it back into the weapon, pulls the slide all the way back, then lets it go, loading a round into the chamber.

"Where is the target?" asks the Jamaican.

"The Cuban official in that building," says Bean as he points to the building on their right. "Do you know a way in around the cameras?"

"Yes," the man says, knowing the Cuban's security will intercept anyone that tries to get on that floor. *I wonder if this stupid American has any more money in that bag,* the Jamaican thinks.

"Will you lead the way?" Bean asks.

The man shakes his head and starts moving towards the building. After a quick stop along the way to pick up a mop, the two men are standing at the back side of a stationary camera focused on an exit door.

"I have a key for the door and will block the camera for a few seconds while we enter," the man informs Bean.

Bean agrees, and the two men walk to the door.

The Jamaican blocks the camera, unlocks the door and they are in.

Once inside, the man requests that Bean take the lead,

and he agrees. Bean is moving slowly up the first flight of stairs when he hears the noise of a cartridge primer going off. When he turns back he sees a surprised Jamaican pointing the Russian-made pistol at him. As Bean stands on the steps looking at him, the man pulls back the receiver and extracts the bad round, loads another and pulls the trigger with the same results.

"I hear men have died because you sold them out," Bean informs him. The Jamaican repeats the process again; he squeezes the trigger, and again the weapon does not fire.

"I think those men deserve a little justice," Bean says still standing there. The man tries a third time, and is bringing the weapon to bear when Bean quickly raises his own weapon and fires twice, hitting the man in the left side of his chest.

Bean walks down the steps, bends and starts picking up the two rounds he had worked on earlier. "Now you know how those men you sold out felt before they lost their lives," he states.

After picking up the rounds, Bean changes back into his green suit and puts his com unit on. He then puts the money back into the resort beach bag, covers it with the towel and puts it on its side next to the man on the floor. Using the Russian weapons, this dead body and all the money will make it look like greed caused a shootout between the Cubans and their agents in Jamaica.

Bean collects the mop, makes a last-second check and moves to the exit door. After adjusting the hood so only his eyes can be seen, Bean opens the door slightly, sticks out the mop so it covers the camera, and quickly moves out and away.

"Back in position," Blue Jay hears over his com unit, and he is on his way to the next floor.

Standing on the balcony railing next to the building's wall, Blue Jay leaps up; eight fingers grasp the floor of the balcony above. Feeling he is getting good gripping power from the gloves, he pulls himself up until he can grab one of the supporting poles of the balcony. That done, he twists to his right and uses the wall to walk up the side of the building until he gets a foothold on the balcony floor above. While holding his position with his left hand, he uses his right to grab the railing, and seconds later he is standing on the balcony.

Bean is still watching the area and Blue Jay at the same time when "Are we still clear?" comes over his com unit. "Still clear," he replies, and then asks, "having any problems?"

"I think my shorts are riding up."

Bean shakes his head and smiles at the answer as he continues his surveillance.

The next floor is Blue Jay's objective, and he shakes his arms to get some fresh blood to his muscles before he starts.

Thirty seconds later, Bean hears "Going for it" on the com, and he starts moving closer to the building.

Blue Jay repeats the procedure, and when he gains the next balcony, he moves to the corner, takes out his weapon and removes the safety.

After standing there a few seconds, he removes a skinny rope that was folded and wrapped around his waist. Holding onto one end, he throws the other end over the balcony and it unfolds to the ground. He then quickly makes a loop with the end he is holding and is about to secure it to the balcony when the door to the balcony opens, and a heavyset man walks out over the objections of voices coming from inside.

Blue Jay immediately recognizes the Cuban. Slowly removing his weapon from its temporary place under his arm he holds it down in front of him and puts his other hand under his suit top.

The Cuban is about to take another puff on his cigar when he notices something has landed next to his left foot. When he looks down, he sees a white rose with the ends of its petals singed. As he turns to his left to pick it up, he sees Blue Jay standing in the corner and is startled. As he moves back, his mouth starts to form a word, but is stopped by two rounds entering his forehead.

The security men inside are quick to react as they jump up and head for the door. Blue Jay is in the doorway before they are, and drops two of them.

The remaining two dive for cover behind furniture and return fire.

Since they're not using silencers their gun fire can be heard loud and clear, alerting other security men. After firing into the doorway, Blue Jay ducks back to his right and the security men fire through the picture windows on either side of the door.

Screw this, thinks Blue Jay, and once again moves to the doorway and fires rounds as fast as he can at the men in the room. With that many rounds coming in, the men duck and Blue Jay puts the loop on the end of the rope over the doorknob and pulls the door shut. Keeping low, firing back through the door and feeding the rope out as he moves, Blue Jay climbs over the railing and lowers himself to the railing on the balcony below, then jumps onto the balcony floor. He moves to the door on that balcony and wraps the rope twice around the new doorknob. That completed, still holding onto the rope, he backtracks and moves the rope, dangling it from the right side of the balconies instead of the front.

The security men are trying to get out the door, but the rope is holding it shut. One of the men starts to climb out the broken picture window, but Bean fires two rounds at him. and they come so close that the man decides to stay inside.

Blue Jay follows the balcony railing around to where it stops just short of touching the back wall, and puts two turns of the rope around it. *This is not sturdy enough, but it will have to do,* he thinks, then after a quick look up towards the upper balcony he is over the railing and rappelling down the rope. As he approaches the second-floor balcony the railing the rope is secured to starts to give. When he is even with the balcony, the railing breaks, putting all of the strain on the third-floor doorknob. With the strain on an angle instead of straight, Blue Jay has a few extra seconds before it also gives in to the pressure. With the rope still attached to the fourth-floor doorknob and Blue Jay still rappelling, the rope snaps like a whip when it straightens out. The remaining doorknob only holds for a few seconds, but Blue Jay is three feet off the ground when it gives. After landing, he moves towards Bean, and then their escape route at the beach. As they approach the beach they see the resort's security force responding to the reports of gunfire.

"They are approaching from the beach, and will intercept anyone trying to flee in their direction," Bean observes.

"Good plan," Blue Jay approves as both men turn and run in the opposite direction, towards the front of the hotel and the long way home.

The Cuban security men are finally on the balcony. Seeing the two men running back towards the building, they open fire on them, but Blue Jay and Bean do not return fire. After the Cubans fire a few more shots a voice amplified by a bull horn instructs the men to cease fire or they will be fired upon. With one look at the six-man hotel security force pointing their weapons at them, the Cubans obey the order.

Bean and Blue Jay are at the halfway point of the long building when they make for the high wall that runs alongside the building, about thirty yards away.

When they reach the wall, Bean stands in a crouched position with his back against it. By interlocking the fingers on each hand with his palms facing up, he creates a step. Blue Jay sees he is ready and takes a few quick strides, puts his foot into the step and at the same time leaps upwards. As he stretches out his body to reach the top, Bean lifts up with his arms and gives him a helping push. Blue Jay manages to get his hand over the top of the wall and a grip on the other side. Between him pulling and Bean pushing his feet, he manages to get on top and sits astride it like a horse.

Grabbing the wall with both legs and bracing his left arm on the other side of the wall, Blue Jay leans down and extends his right arm down to his partner. Bean goes into a deep knee bend, then quickly straightens up and reaches for the extended arm. At the same moment they grab each others' arms, and Blue Jay helps him get to the top of the wall. With both men now on top, they jump to the other side and continue their escape.

When they reach the road in front of the resort, they have to go down into a gully, then up the other side before they can cross the road. One of the Cuban security men isn't giving up the chase, and has guessed what direction they would be taking. When Blue Jay and Bean attempt to go up the other side of the gully, the Cuban opens fire with an AK-47, nearly hitting both of them. The men retreat back into the gully and out of sight. While they are trying to calculate their next move, the Cuban climbs onto a car parked inside the resort so he can get a better shot at them. Once he is standing on the roof of the car, he starts firing into the gully.

In the middle of his second burst, he loses his footing and falls backwards off the roof of the car.

Bean and Blue Jay see what has just happened, scramble out of the gully and across the road. Keeping low, their green suits blend right into the undergrowth. They travel fast, and soon the two men are out of the area and moving toward the secondary extraction point, a long walk away.

"I wonder what happened to that guy on the roof of the car?" Bean says.

"Want to go back and ask him?"

"No," Bean replies. "I'll ask him next time."

Five hundred yards off the resort property, a man is lying in the bushes with a Russian sniper rifle. Watching through his scope, he sees the two men have escaped into the underbrush. He removes the rifle from his shoulder, looks at it and mutters, "This AK Sniper Rifle is jolly good!"

CHAPTER SEVENTEEN

I t has been a long day at the office for Swabbie.
Grumbling from the State Department about Nicaragua has
generated a message to the DDO. Dunn received the message and,
replacing a few key points with his own editing, it reads:

"A prominent resident (gun-running dope dealer) of Nicaragua
was assassinated, and one of his warehouses containing millions of
dollars of company property (guns and dope) was also destroyed."

The message from State was pretty good up to that point--then it
added: "The Ambassador to Nicaragua is flying back to Washington,
and wants us to tell you to keep yourself available in case she wants
to interview you on the matter."

It took Dunn's secretary a while to peel him off of the ceiling, but
when she did, his first call was to Swabbie. They both knew going
into their meeting that the Agency was not officially involved with
the Nicaragua episode, but reviewed it anyway.

After discussing it for a few minutes, Dunn raised a question
about Bean and Blue Jay's fishing trip.

Swabbie admits he had the same thought, but reminds the DDO
he had people follow them and they had watched the boat leave the
dock.

Dunn acknowledges the statement, but says he would feel a lot
better if they could get in touch with the two of them far out to sea.

It was late in the afternoon when Swabbie assured the DDO he
would get right on it...but so far has been unable to reach the boat.
The people that rented the boat informed him the last time they
communicated with them was the morning they departed, and that
transmissions from the boat were broken up and had a lot of static.

From that moment on, his suspicions started to grow.

At 9 p.m., Swabbie calls home and tells Anne he is just leaving
work, and will be getting something to eat along the way.

"Long day?" inquires Anne.

"Very," answers Swabbie.

"I can tell," she informs him, then after additional small talk they
hang up.

Swabbie decides to go to the Top of the Town for a light dinner. It's in a high-rise that sits on a hill behind the Marine Corps Memorial. Being that high up gives him a good view of Washington, D.C., and a place to think.

When Swabbie gets to the restaurant he bypasses valet parking and looks for a spot on the street. He goes another block and lucks out. After parking his car, he starts walking back towards the restaurant. It is a residential neighborhood, and does not have the bright lighting of the streets in downtown D.C. Between thinking and watching where he is going, Swabbie isn't paying attention to his surroundings.

When he is half a block from his destination, a man suddenly appears in front of him from out of nowhere.

Swabbie is startled at first, but then starts to check the surroundings and notices another man to his left across the street, and one about the same distance behind him.

"Don't be alarmed, *senor*," the man assures him, speaking with a Latino accent. "We need to talk."

"And them?" Swabbie asks, gesturing towards the other two men.

"My sons," the man explains. "You will understand after we speak. Let me start by refreshing your memory," the man continues. "You have never met me, but you did meet my sons when they were both children."

The man continues his story, and he and Swabbie start slowly walking as he talks.

"Think back to when you were a field operative with your two friends, and the Cubans were in Nicaragua. You and your two friends were sent to the island of Cayos to hunt down a man and his group that had become Cuban operatives. You were accompanied by a local four-man kill squad, and were instructed to eliminate the threat. When you found my home, I was not there, but my wife and sons were.

After talking it over amongst themselves, the kill squad wanted to terminate my family. You objected, but the kill squad insisted and threatened you as well. My sons thought they would never see their father again, but then you and your friends challenged the squad. It erupted into gunfire, and within seconds the kill squad members were dead."

"I remember," Swabbie says as he looks at the two handsome young men. "And your wife?" he asks.

"Very well, thank you for asking," answers the Latino.

"One of the reasons I wanted to speak with you is this," the man continues. "I was loyal to my cause for many years, but now I see it is decaying badly. In the beginning there was honor, but now there is just an empty, corrupted regime. I am sick of it and I am taking my family away from it all, but before I depart I had to repay you for saving my family."

Swabbie tries to assure him there is no need, but the Latino insists.

"You have a traitor associated with your organization," he relays to Swabbie. "This man does not do it for cause or conviction; he does it for money and only money." The Latino's voice is infused with anger. "People have lost their lives because of this man, and it was all for *dinero*. This man is also the one responsible for setting up your friends-not once, but twice."

"How do you know these things?" inquires Swabbie.

"He passed information about other matters to me, and after the Nicaragua incident I started making inquires and discovered he was the source."

The two men walk and talk for awhile about other things; then the Latino introduced Swabbie to his sons, who thank him for saving their mother and themselves many years before.

"Very nice young men," Swabbie compliments them and their father. "If I can help with your relocation, or anything else, please let me know."

The men thank him, bid him farewell, and then again disappear into the night.

Swabbie decides to bypass the restaurant, and returns to his car. After a stop at Dunn's house, he heads for home and a midnight snack with Anne.

***

The next day, Swabbie and Dunn are at the office bright and early. They are joined by Di Flipi, an intelligence analyst that works closely with the DDO. They have to verify that what the Latino told Swabbie last night is true, and not just misinformation to throw the Agency into turmoil.

All three men have cleared their plates, and will focus completely on this project. With one of them on the case, verification one way or the other is a sure thing. With all three of them involved, it will be done three times as fast.

During the meeting, Dunn tells Swabbie, "The information the Latino gave you last night helped verify our findings. Di Flipi had a suspicion; we went with it and it looks like he was right, as usual. This is from my private file. Only Di Flipi and myself have seen it," Dunn finishes as he hands a folder over to Swabbie,

Swabbie pages through the documents and notes, while Dunn and

Di Flipi retrieve three cups of coffee from the coffeemaker in the office. After working together for so many years, Dunn knows how Swabbie likes it: half a sugar and a little cream.

Swabbie is a fast reader, especially when it comes to something this important, and is three quarters of the way through the documents when Dunn goes to refill his coffee cup.

A short time later, Swabbie sits back in his chair and Dunn can see the wheels start to spin.

"This explains a lot," are Swabbie's first words.

"To say the least," confirms Dunn. "And as you can see, the time frames the Latino gave you coincide with the dates in my file."

"Right on the money," Swabbie agrees.

"I was a little surprised about the motive," Dunn adds, then volunteers to look for a money trail.

Dunn, Swabbie and Di Flipi each select items to check out, and agree to meet back in Dunn's office at one o'clock.

Swabbie, Di Flipi and Dunn are very intense for the rest of the day. Gert has picked up on it. She knows something is up and asks Swabbie what is going on, but he says, "Nothing Gert, just the same old, same old."

'Same old,' my ass, Gert thinks as she smiles and returns to her desk.

At 1 p.m., Swabbie and Di Flipi are seated in Dunn's office sharing their findings.

"He has a pile of money in an offshore account," Dunn offers. "Even used our techniques for keeping the account unknown."

"His style of living is a little on the high side, but nothing to make anyone take notice," Swabbie adds. "He used his head and stayed just inside his means when it came to money. He was probably waiting for the day when he could safely use the money he earned betraying all of those people. Well, if it is him, that payday is not going to happen, " Swabbie continues.

An hour later, the three have shared all of their information, put it together with Dunn's file and the Latino's information, and know they have the right person.

"Look at these travel dates. Most are prior to failed projects and/or people losing their lives," Dunn announces as he throws the paper back onto his desk.

The three men continue their analysis for another hour, then Dunn states, "We have enough, I'll get things started."

Swabbie and Di Flipi shake their heads in agreement as Dunn goes out and asks his secretary to make arrangements for a meeting in his office at four o'clock with his immediate subordinate, General

Wallace.

When he returns he instructs Di Flipi to get in touch with the FBI liaison to the Agency and fill him in on everything. It will be their responsibility to get a warrant and an arrest.

The conversation briefly changes to the lost lives and failed projects because of one person's greed, then the meeting breaks up and Di Flipi goes to contact the FBI liaison while Swabbie returns to his office.

***

At 3:45 Swabbie and Gert approach the DDO's secretary. After exchanging pleasantries, Swabbie suggests that he and the secretary take a walk to catch up on things before she goes on extended leave.

"I'd love to, but General Wallace is arriving at four o'clock for a meeting," the secretary apologizes.

"I think Gert would be happy to fill in for you," Swabbie offers, and Gert is quick to agree.

The secretary looks at them both for a few seconds, then asks, "Rumble in the city?" as she gestures towards Dunn's office.

"Maybe," Swabbie replies.

"Under different circumstances I would want to stay, but I don't think I need any excitement right now," she admits as she pushes her chair away from the desk and stands up.

"It looks like it is going to be a boy to me," Swabbie announces.

"Kicks like one," she comments as she and Swabbie start their stroll.

***

At 4 p.m., General Wallace and his aide, Captain Zack, arrive, and Gert informs the general to go right in. As both men start towards the door, Gert speaks up: "Excuse me, General; the DDO would like to see you alone, if you don't mind."

"But, sir," the captain starts to register a complaint, but is interrupted by Gert saying, "Your aide can have a seat over there," as she points to several chairs arranged around a small table filled with magazines.

"No problems, Captain," the general says, giving him a look that says *I can handle this punk.*

The captain retreats to the waiting area as the general enters the office and closes the door behind him.

"What's so urgent, Dunn?" inquires the general in a voice of authority. He uses this voice to put the person he's talking to on guard. It never has worked with Dunn, but he keeps trying.

"Have a seat," Dunn offers, gesturing to a chair directly in front of his desk.

After sitting in the chair the general exclaims, "Well."

"Read this," the DDO orders as he places a folder on the other side of his desk in front of the General.

Acting unimpressed, the general picks up the folder, opens it and begins to read. As he reads the documents in the folder, the arrogant attitude gives way to one of concern, then disbelief.

"Is this all true?" he inquires.

"Done most of the investigating myself," Dunn assures him.

"What will we do about this?"

"I'm glad you asked that," Dunn replies. "First of all, as my subordinate, this matter fell into your area of responsibility, but you were so busy playing politics in an effort to get my position that you were not doing your job, and as a result all of this happened."

"I hope you don't try to make me a scapegoat for this," says the general, starting to regain his composure. "I have friends in high places."

"Scapegoat?" Dunn repeats. "No, I just want you out of here. Now, this is what is going to happen: You are going back to your office and submit your papers for retirement.

"Now, I realize all of this was allowed to happen because you where busy playing politics and are a total incompetent, but if you don't put in for your retirement, I have a feeling an article will show up in the New York Times implicating you in this mess, and I will make it look like you were involved."

"You're forgetting my friends," the general reminds Dunn.

"Fuck you and your friends in high places," Dunn explodes. "You know as well as I do that those rat bastards will drop you like a hot potato two seconds after the newspapers hit the stands."

The general has never been dressed down like this before, and his anger is reaching its max as he throws the folder back on Dunn's desk. "Who do you think you're talking to?" he demands.

"I'm talking to a pompous ass that built a career by kissing ass and playing politics in Washington."

That statement puts the general over the top, and he lunges out of his chair and takes a swing at Dunn's face. Dunn doesn't even flinch as he blocks the attack with his left arm, then delivers a short punch with his right hand that lands underneath his nose and extends down to his jaw, driving the general back into his seat.

The commotion can be heard outside the office, and as the captain stands up he inquires, "What was that?"

"What was what?" Gert inquires.

"The commotion from inside the office," he replies.

It is again quiet in the DDO's office and Gert replies, "I don't hear anything. Have a seat."

The captain starts to insist, and Gert changes her expression from smiling secretary to her chasing-a-mugger face, and the captain returns to his seat.

A few seconds pass, the office door opens and the general rushes out, holding a handkerchief to his mouth to absorb a little blood seeping from his teeth.

After the two men have departed and are walking quickly down the hall, the DDO appears in the doorway and says, "Thanks Gert."

"Any time, Gil," Gert replies as the two exchange big smiles.

***

Dunn's secretary and Swabbie are still taking their stroll when the DDO's intercom rings. "Yes, Gert?" Dunn inquires.

"I see more company coming your way," Gert informs him. "The Ambassador to Nicaragua."

"This must be my lucky day," he replies in an upbeat voice. "Send her right in."

When she arrives with her Agency security escort, Gert ushers the ambassador into the office, and as she closes the door thinks, *This is the second pompous ass to pass through this doorway in the past hour.*

After taking a seat, the Ambassador goes on the attack. "Since you didn't make yourself available to be interviewed by me, I was forced to come here."

"And?" Dunn inquires.

The Ambassador is a little disturbed by his lack of concern, and the conversation grows brisk.

"*And,* I thought I made it clear that Nicaragua was off-limits to the CIA."

"Who are you to tell the CIA anything?" Dunn fires back. "if it wasn't for your family being a member of the political in-crowd, you would be just another rich bitch looking for a life."

"Well, I see this was a waste of time," she replies, her anger rising, "I came here to…"

"You came here impersonating a U.S. Ambassador," Dunn cuts off her statement.

With that, the Ambassador jumps up and starts to leave the office. When she gets by the office door she turns and says, "You will regret this. I'll start with my political contacts, but if I have to I'll go to the newspapers to bring you down."

"If you hurry, you'll be able to get something in tomorrow's Washington Post. Maybe a spot next to the article about how the Ambassador to Nicaragua, through her political contacts in

Washington, put restrictions on the CIA that prevented them from stopping an attempted coup in Nicaragua by a wealthy gun-running dope dealer and the Cuban government."

The Ambassador is caught totally off guard by Dunn's revelations, and before she can recover he adds "This is just a guess, but it looks to me like you're going back to being just another rich bitch looking for a life."

That last statement redlines the Ambassador's anger. She turns the doorknob and swings the door open so hard it crashes into the wall as she leaves the office.

Seconds later, Gert is in the doorway, and as she starts to close the door asks, "Another satisfied customer?"

Dunn gives Gert a big smile as he shakes his head yes.

CHAPTER EIGHTEEN

T he streets in Georgetown are busy, for a rainy night: people out for dinner, tourists taking in the sights and the usual Georgetown crowd.

A man in his forties is just leaving a liquor store on Wisconsin Avenue, carrying a very expensive bottle of brandy--nothing but the best for this man. As he navigates through the sidewalk traffic, he protects the brown paper bag containing the brandy like a running back protects the football on a Sunday afternoon.

Across the street, in the shadows, a man is watching, and when the man with the bag starts walking down Wisconsin Avenue he removes something from his pocket. After looking around his immediate area, to make sure no one is near, he opens his hand to reveal a small cylinder that is a little bit longer than the width of his palm. One end of the cylinder is plain-looking, but the other end appears as though a bullet is attached to it; part of the casing and the entire projectile can be seen. A lever that resembles a spoon handle runs from just under the bullet to halfway down the cylinder. If the safety apparatus is not in place and the lever is squeezed, it causes a firing pin to strike the back end of the bullet, firing the primer; the power will ignite and the projectile will be launched off the end of the casing. Since the bullet does not travel through a gun barrel, the projectile travels end over end, with devastating results when it finds its mark.

It is a crude device, but very effective at close range, and there is little ballistic evidence left behind. The man removes the safety and replaces it with the fingers of his right hand. He then puts his right hand into his raincoat pocket.

The seam of the pocket has been cut, and allows his hand to pass through it and into the pocket of his sport jacket.

The man then moves out of the shadows, walks across the street and quickens his pace to close the distance between himself and the man with the brown bag. Two blocks later, the gap has been closed and he is waiting for the right opportunity.

When the man with the bag is waiting at the corner of Wisconsin

Avenue and M Street for the light to turn green, the man following notices a D.C. bus that has just loaded its last rider and the doors of the bus are closing.

He moves the fingers of his right hand from under to over the lever, and moves slowly forward. The bus still has the green light and starts to pull away from the curb, its diesel engine roaring as the vehicle picks up speed. As the bus approaches, the man slowly raises his right arm and squeezes the lever. The projectile tears through the sport jacket's pocket and into the man carrying the brandy, propelling him in front of the bus. Between the projectile and the impact of the bus, Colonel Monet, General Wallace's assistant, is dead in a matter of seconds. The man in the raincoat removes his left hand from the other pocket and holds a handkerchief over his nose and mouth in reaction to the man getting hit by the bus. He then turns away and slowly moves to the back of the crowd that is starting to form.

Still holding the handkerchief up to his face, he moves slowly down the street and stands close to an alleyway. Seconds later, he is gone.

CHAPTER NINETEEN

A Seal Team has been dispatched to retrieve two men from the island. They have been in place waiting for some time when the two men finally appear. The Seal Team Leader appears out of nowhere and informs them, "The DDO has sent us to escort you out of the area."

"It's him again," the two men exclaim, recognizing the Seal Team Leader from Sardinia.

"It's what we do, Sir," replies the Navy Lieutenant before he speaks into his com unit and instructs their high-speed boat to approach and take everyone aboard.

***

Two days have passed when Blue Jay and Bean are sitting outside the DDO's office, waiting to be called in.

"This should be interesting," Bean says to Blue Jay in a low voice.

"Screw 'em," is Blue Jay's reply.

"You and this problem with management," Bean observes.

As Bean is ending his observation, the door to the

DDO's office swings open and Dunn escorts the Seal Team Leader out. "I wanted to thank you in person, Lieutenant, for your help in getting my men off that island."

"Thank you, Sir; can I relay that to the Team?" the Lieutenant asks.

"By all means." Dunn gives his hearty approval and again shakes hands with the Seal Team Leader.

"You're next," Dunn says as he points to Blue Jay and Bean, then goes back into his office.

"It's him again," Blue Jay says as he and Bean approach the Lieutenant,

"Thanks again," Bean offers, then before the Seal Team Leader can respond Bean and Blue Jay sing out, "Yeah, we know, it's what you do."

"That's about it," the Lieutenant quickly replies.

"And we are both glad it is what you do," Blue Jay and Bean

reassure him as they shake hands with him, then continue into the DDO's office.

When Bean and Blue Jay enter the office, they see Dunn has assembled a small group of men, and they seem to be waiting for them.

An inquisition or a tribunal are their first two thoughts as they scan the group. At first glance, from the back, they can tell the man to the far left is Swabbie, but before they can check out the others the questioning is in process.

"What have you children been up to?"

For once, neither Blue Jay nor Bean can think of anything to say.

"I never thought I would see the day when both of them would be at a loss for words," Jar Head observes.

"I know," agrees Doggie. "What is this world coming to?"

Bean and Blue Jay try to recover, with words like *how* and *what*...but mostly, *how*?!

"Have a seat, and we'll fill you in," Jar Head announces.

When both men are seated, Doggie starts filling them in on how they managed to survive.

"It was really a team effort and a lot of luck. When I saw the man with the flame thrower I figured our time was up, but I was determined to take some of them with us. I wrapped some tape from the first aid kit around some grenades to hold the spoons down, pulled the pins and tossed them out in front of our position."

Then Jar Head picks up the explanation, "After throwing some loose rounds out in the same area for the same reason, I took out my trusty entrenching tool and started to dig at the base of the palm tree. When Doggie was done with the grenades, he also started digging."

"It's amazing how fast you can dig when you know a man with a flame thrower is on the way," adds Doggie. When the hole was finished, we squeezed into it and used the tools to pull as much sand as we could over our bodies. That done, we placed our backpacks over our faces. Holding on to them with one hand and our MP-5s with the other, we waited."

"We didn't have to wait long," Jar Head announces. "It was getting hot as hell-and we figured that was the ball game--when we felt the ground shake from an exploding grenade. That took out the flame man, and he sprayed others as he fell. Two of the poor souls tried to run to the water, but didn't make it."

"Were they the ones Jack saw that night he visited the island, when he thought the bodies were you two?" asks Bean.

"Yes," Doggie confirms. "After that happened they assumed we were dead anyway, and they didn't know how many grenades were getting ready to explode, so they called off any further action."

"And not a moment too soon," Jar Head explains. "Our packs were on fire, and we had to get rid of them before the flames ate all the way through. We threw the packs away, decided to crawl for the surf, then started moving further down the beach. We got away from the area in case the main man left anyone behind to check things out in the morning."

"Having been on that island before, and with our backpacks and com gear destroyed, we made our way to some friendlies we knew from years ago. It took us a long time, but we finally found them."

"I can pick it up from there," Swabbie volunteers.

"During that prior visit, the three of us saved a man's family from a death squad. Wanting to repay that debt, he and his sons got in touch with me and told me, along with other things, that Doggie and Jar Head were safe. He gave me the location where they could be picked up, and Gil sent the Seal Team."

"To start with, he is an honorable man, but he was getting disgusted with the things he was seeing," Jar Head adds. "He told us that for years he did not want to except the fact that what he believed in was becoming so corrupted that it didn't even resemble anything from the old days. He was in the process of moving his family to another place, and if we had arrived two days later, we wouldn't have found them."

"Now that you're all caught up, it's my turn," Dunn announces. "By working to get the schedule moved up, Colonel Monet caused a domino affect that brought down things he was not even aware of."

"And you two have to be the luckiest men on the planet. You went from a possible stay at Leavenworth to smelling like roses. Oh, you were doing pretty good until you followed the Cuban to Jamaica, and our business jet had to land at Montego Bay airport.

"I know the real reason you went after those two, but in doing so you prevented a coup that was planned for the following week, and you stopped the drug trafficking that was supplying the funds to the organization that wanted to take over Nicaragua. You did go way out of bounds, and will have to be disciplined. I order you two back into training until further notice.

"The only thing unanswered is, who took out Colonel Monet?" Dunn continues. "Was it you two?" he says, looking at Blue Jay and Bean, then answers his own question with, "No it couldn't have been. You were still playing 'catch me, fuck me' with the DDO when that happened."

"Maybe it was your secretary, Blue Jay offers. "She *is* pregnant, and those hormonal things can get out of hand sometimes."

"How can you say something like that?" Bean scolds. "This is what I think happened. Monet stepped in front of the bus, and the bus driver shot him because he put a dent in his vehicle."

Dunn just looks at the two men, then at Jar Head, and instructs, "Put my name on the list. I want to know when a house becomes available at the Village."

Then Dunn assumes the role of the DDO again and instructs Swabbie: "Take this circus out of here so I can catch up on my work."

As everyone is leaving his office, the DDO informs Blue Jay and Bean, "Since you two are on a lucky streak, maybe you should go to a casino. And take all of your helpers with you. They seem to be on lucky streaks as well."

Due to their leg wounds, Doggie and Jar Head are walking with canes, and the five men move slowly down the hall. Dunn is watching from his office doorway, waiting for the chatter he knows is going to start.

The three older men are leading with the other two walking behind when Jar Head fires the opening volley.

"So, we have to start training them again. Like getting shot wasn't punishment enough."

"Well, you spoiled them," Doggie insists.

After a brief pause, Bean starts the return salvo.

"Oh, joy, we're going to be stuck with these two old farts again."

"Tell me about it," Blue Jay says. "I wonder how long they'll be milking this cane routine?"

Dunn shakes his head and laughs as Blue Jay and Bean continue the verbal jousting with Their Agency Fathers.